About the author

I was born and raised in Germany in a town close to the Dutch border. I studied Germanistik at Műnster University, where I met my husband who served in the British Army in 1988. On his retirement, we settled in a small village on the outskirts of the Saddlewoth Moors. This is my debut novel.

THE UNIFORM

P E White

The Uniform

Vanguard Press

VANGUARD PAPERBACK

© Copyright 2020
P E White

A CIP catalogue record for this title is
available from the British Library.

ISBN 978 1 78465 740 6

Vanguard Press is an imprint of
Pegasus Elliot MacKenzie Publishers Ltd.
www.pegasuspublishers.com

First Published in 2020

Vanguard Press
Sheraton House Castle Park
Cambridge England

Printed & Bound in Great Britain

Acknowledgements

Thank you for reading my first attempt at writing. If you read to the end I hope you enjoyed it. At the beginning, my story was going to be a murder mystery. However, it became pretty clear early on that I was going to write a book incorporating my own experiences as a young army wife and the story developed from there. It was a labour of love and to be totally truthful a little bit of therapy.

I would like to thank my best friend since school, Jutta Overbeck who exclaimed one day sitting outside a café in my German hometown, that I was a good storyteller and should write a book. At the time I thought it was ludicrous. Nobody just writes a book on a whim, right?

With the encouragement of my 'sister from another mister', Maggie Hansford, I would never have had the courage to actually put pen to paper. Thank you for being my friend.

Thanks to all the people who read the manuscript and their valuable ideas and constructive criticism, especially Helen Batty, who read my first draft, and Olwyn White, who read my last. I'll be forever grateful for your opinions and feedback.

Thanks to Vicky Gorry of Pegasus Elliot Mackenzie Publishers, who always steered me through my wobbles and tantrums, back into calmer waters. I couldn't have asked for a better advisor.

Special thanks to my husband, who has been my inspiration for Jonathan. Although the story is fictional, he actually served in Iraq and came back to me. Thank you for your patience.

Last but not least; although I have tried to stay as close to real events and locations whilst writing my book it was not always possible to be one hundred percent accurate so I had to use my poetic licence. I do apologize if I got it wrong in places and hope I am not going to be judged on those parts.

Any resemblance of characters in the book to persons known, living or deceased is unintentional.

Thank you for showing an interest in my story and thank you for giving me your time.

Trish 06.02.2019

'Life puts us on a path no matter where we are born in the world. Whether we stay on that path is a different story.'

For Tim

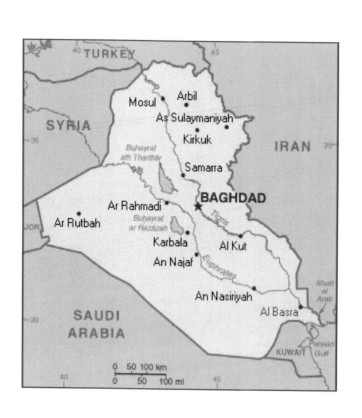

Prologue

The man looked at his wife over the edge of the newspaper in his hands. She was busy preparing their evening meal at the stove, humming to an old Beatles song playing on the radio. The air in the kitchen was heavy with the scent of cinnamon and star anise and he could almost taste the tartness of the lemons in the stew cooking on the hob. His eyes travelled from the back of her head down her spine over her perfectly proportioned bottom to her thin ankles and tiny feet. He sighed. He loved this woman with all that he possessed.

He loves to look into her black eyes, that are full of warmth and humour. When she cries, he loves her for her compassion. He loves to stroke her shiny raven hair, that would fall to the bottom of her spine when she wore it untied in the house. It was beginning to show strands of grey but he loves to run his fingers through those strands. He loves the grace in which she moves, her kindness and patience. He adores her smile. She has retained her figure and although there are a few wrinkles around her eyes he doesn't care. She is his.

They've been married almost twenty-five years but he had known her for almost all his life. Without noticing when exactly, she had put a spell on him and he knew he was going to marry her when she was of age. He used to watch her performing her chores at the banks of the river after school when he hunted for fish with her brother. He would carry the washing for her when she finished and her brother teased him for it, calling him names. He let it go because her brother was his best friend. He would bring her little gifts, glass pebbles that he found washed up on the river bank. These looked dull when they were dry but once they were immersed in water they would shimmer like jewels. He told her he would give her real jewels one day.

Once he found a beautiful flower and when he handed it to her, he told her that she was more beautiful than any flower in the world. Sitting at the riverbank he dared to hold her tiny hand in his. He told her that he would marry her and she shyly smiled that sweet smile. He'd had to admire her from afar then, serving the food, walking around the men with grace and elegance, as he sat together with his friend after prayers on a Friday evening at her father's house. It seemed such a long time ago. She was ten and he was almost sixteen.

She turned around and smiled at him. A warm feeling of pride entered his heart. 'Yes,' he thought. 'I made the right choices.' He smiled back at her and continued to read.

His eyes scanned over an article in the paper. He held the newspaper closer to his eyes and reached for his glasses. Had he read it right? The colour drained from his face. He folded the paper together and stood up.

'I'm just going for a smoke, my love,' he said.

She turned around, looked at the paper he had tucked under his arm. 'Where're you going with that? I haven't had a chance to look at it yet,' she said.

'Mrs Dean from the library told me there are money-off vouchers in there today. Everything is going to be half price in M&S on Saturday so I need those. I was going to cut them out after dinner.'

He drew a sharp breath and laid the paper back on the table. He opened it in the middle, found the coupons, ripped the page out and handed it to her. She took it from him with a questioning look.

'There you go, are you happy now?' he replied and stepped outside, instantly regretting his harsh words. He walked over to the gate and threw the paper in the recycling bin at the back of their house.

There he stood, lit a cigarette and blew the smoke into the evening sky. The sound of a window being opened ripped him from his thoughts.

'Dinner is ready if you are interested,' she shouted at him from above. He sighed and stubbed the cigarette out on the floor.

She put a plate of steaming food in front of him. He pulled her towards him and took her hand.

'I'm sorry for the way I spoke to you earlier,' he said and kissed the inside of her hand. 'I just had a bad day today. Can you forgive me?'

She looked at him still sulking but then she smiled and he sighed with relief.

'I forgive you. You can talk to me about anything, you know.'

But he kept quiet. So, she sat down next to him and they shared the meal she had lovingly prepared.

1.

It was a day like any other day.

The alarm bell rang exactly ten minutes before her husband had to get up for work. Enough time to put some bread in the toaster and make him a cup of tea for the long drive to wherever he was working today.

Inga had broken her leg the previous year in a freak accident on the Yorkshire coast. Her husband Jonathan thought it would be a good idea to take a closer look at the seals at the bottom of the cliff. It would have been a great experience if she hadn't turned over on her ankle close to the beach. Her scream scared off all the seals and her cries were probably heard all the way back to Scarborough. After Jonathan managed to stop laughing, he made her wiggle her toes and gave her his diagnosis that the leg wasn't broken.

'I heard it snap you fool,' she'd shouted between sobs, her face covered in tears and snot which made him laugh again.

'It sounded like a twig being snapped in half. I can't make it back up to the top. Can you ring the coastguard to pick me up?'

A family passed where she sat crying and offered to help. Inga squirmed with embarrassment.

'If it's sprained you need to get back up to the top as soon as possible,' the woman said.

Jonathan gave her two choices. He could ring for help or they could try and make it on their own. Inga thought about it for two seconds.

'I'm not being winched up into an air ambulance to be shown on Yorkshire television tonight,' she exclaimed. 'God, how embarrassing,' Inga said, wiping her eyes and blowing her nose into a piece of TESCO till receipt. She looked at the family with their children on the beach below.

'I gave birth to two children for God's sake. How hard can it be?'
Two hours later she thought that giving birth had been so easy in
comparison.

As it turned out, two days later, she had broken her fibula. Being in
plaster for six weeks and having a lot of time to think and re-evaluate her
life, she decided not to return to work.

Even before Inga broke her leg, she felt that life was a struggle. She
got up to go to work, shopped at dinnertime. She looked in on her
daughter who struggled with cranial hypertension, which had resulted in
her hospitalisation twice to reduce the pressure on her brain. Inga often
stayed at her desk and worked through lunch. She could have gone home
at five but instead worked late. The usual household tasks were still
waiting for her when she returned home. She felt like she was running
around organising everyone else's life. She had suffered from bouts of
depression all her life but at that time was struggling daily to keep her
shit together. Medication had helped with the symptoms for a while just
so she could function like a normal human being, but the feeling of self-
loathing and worthlessness surfaced again after she stopped taking the
pills. There had to be another way.

Giving up work wasn't a decision she made lightly. Inga had
sleepless nights for months before gaining enough courage to speak to
her husband. Having been given the all-clear from a cancer scare made
her realise that life was too short. Jonathan was very understanding when
she approached the issue on the day before her tumble in August. When
she fell down the cliff and broke her leg she decided it had been divine
intervention. She was very fortunate because her husband had a well paid
job, she was grateful and for that she was going to make it work.

She re-acquainted herself with various hobbies, started knitting,
sewing and baking. Her new doctor explored the possibility of a hormone
deficiency and prescribed HRT. She started to feel the difference within
a couple of weeks. It made her wonder if she had been suffering a
hormone imbalance all her life. To her it felt like a miracle. Over time
the depressed person she had become changed for the better and she
looked forward to getting up in the mornings. In January her son had
flown the nest and moved halfway around the world. She was very sad

but looked forward to finally having some 'alone' time with her husband. Mostly she looked forward to finding a way back to herself.

The dog also benefitted greatly. Now, uncharacteristically after all these years, she started taking him out for long walks. Toby couldn't wait to see her put her shoes on and reach for the lead.

It was an unusually wet spring this year but the days were getting longer. Inga hoped for a better summer than the previous year. As usual the forecasters were promising a record heatwave but she didn't believe in all that hype. She didn't expect it to last beyond the first week of May. She moved to the north west of England, right beside the Penines and as a rule the only weather to talk about was rain. Light rain, heavy rain, rain disguised as sleet and snow, downpours. Sometimes the clouds were so heavy with moisture that she couldn't see the top of the houses on the hill at the back of her garden. Most days she could not remember why she decided to settle here of all places when her husband had retired from the army after twenty-two years' service.

But on a nice day, when the sun came out from behind the clouds and the rays touched the heather on the moors turning the ground into a vivid purple, when the clear blue skies were in stark contrast to the lush green hills, when the newborn lambs, white as snow, frolicked next to their mothers, when the rugged landscape with the old stone farmhouses looked as pretty as a picture, on those days she considered herself lucky to live in such beautiful surroundings.

Not many people were out walking their dogs on the path this morning. Exchanging pleasant 'Good mornings' with them, she walked under the bridge, listening to the echo of her footsteps and the morning traffic above. She passed the local allotments every day and it made her smile. Some of the wooden sheds looked like apartments for poultry, painted in striking red, white ladders leaning at a comfortable angle for the chickens to climb. She listened to the cockerels, crowing their hearts out. Some managed better than others. At that moment, one of them sounded like it was being strangled halfway through its call.

'He will never impress a hen crowing like that,' she giggled.

When she was a little girl, growing up in Germany, her Opa (grandfather) had kept chickens and rabbits and Inga helped to look after them. She fed them after school, collected the eggs and cleaned their cages. She had brushed her favourite rabbit's fur till it shone. Her Opa entered it into the local breeder competition. It won a rosette. She had been devastated when she realised that the same rabbit had landed on her plate.

'That's life,' her Opa said as a matter of fact. He died not long after. She was ten.

They lived in a three-bedroom flat, which her parents rented from the railway company her father worked for. Her mother was a hairdresser. Her grandparents on her father's side lived in the flat upstairs. Inga was the oldest of three and had to share the bedroom with her sister and brother.

It was nice to have her grandparents living upstairs because they also had a dog. He was a brilliant dog and she loved him very much. When her grandfather died and her parents gave the dog away and sold the rabbits and chickens, it broke her heart. Her father said that he didn't have the time to care for the animals, nobody thought to ask her opinion. Instead, her papa showed her how to grow potatoes, tomatoes, beans, carrots and lettuce along with some more exotic vegetables. They had rows of fruit trees, apples and pears and at the entrance of the garden was a large cherry tree, which looked pretty in the spring, covered in pink petals. Her mother was never short of a bunch of flowers for her front room.

As Inga skipped through memory lane, remembering her childhood, she wondered how hard it would be to apply for her own little plot. They had a garden at the back of the house but it was a place for strawberries in hanging baskets, and single plants in flowerpots; for sipping wine on the wooden patio on a summer's evening, weather permitting of course. The ground was covered in fake grass and she laughed at the squirrels trying to hide their nuts in autumn, digging a pretend hole and dropping the nut on the floor. She would love to go back to nature, grow her own vegetables and keep chickens like her grandfather had done.

She resolutely lifted her head and to the dismay of the dog, cut her walk short. She decided to give the council a ring. Inga didn't hold much hope when she picked up the phone and dialled the local number. She had friends who had been on a waiting list for years trying to get one of those plots. After a short conversation which led her to believe exactly that, she left her details with the lady at the council and resigned herself on a long wait.

However, to her surprise the telephone rang two weeks later. A lease had become available at short notice. Nobody in front of her on the list was either willing, or able to take it on. The lady on the phone didn't go into much detail, only to say that it was a big project. Inga accepted without hesitation and signed the necessary paperwork a few days later. She picked up the keys and made her way down the little lane leading to her assigned plot.

When she stepped out of the car and looked through a hole in the fence it became apparent as to why nobody had been willing to take this plot. She braced herself. The previous owner had neglected the place with utter disregard to its purpose. It was unbelievable how the neighbouring owners didn't complain earlier. Then again, they were possibly unaware since the fence surrounding the plot was six foot high, maybe even higher. Inga unlocked the gate with the key that was given to her and pushed. Nothing. She looked around. At the far end of the fence seemed to be a gap she might be able to fit through. Inga was neither slim nor athletic. She had put on quite a few pounds since she stopped working.

Maybe one too many glasses of Prosecco and slices of cake. She was hardly a friend of exercise.

Inga looked at the two panels in front of her. 'Here goes nothing,' she said to the gap in the fence. 'They will have a good laugh if I get stuck and have to be rescued by the fire brigade.'

She put one foot through the hole and squeezed her frame sideways through the gap. At one point she thought she was not going to be able to make it after all and broke out in a cold sweat. She heard the panel behind her bottom crack. Inga turned her body and forced her rather large chest through the panel in front of her. She flung herself forward but she was going nowhere. Looking down she saw the bottom of her trousers stuck on a rusty nail. Panicking, she started to pull her leg. There was a sharp ripping noise and all of a sudden she found herself free, and turned her body just in time, landing on her hands and knees in the mud.

'That went well, didn't it?' she mumbled under her breath. Getting up on one knee, then on the other, she wiped the mud of her hands and looked up.

The first thing that struck her was the sheer size of the grounds. It was enormous. In the absence of an owner, teenagers, no doubt, had used the plot to meet up on weekends to party. There was a two-seater car chair propped up against the back of the gate. Bottles of beer, cider and Coke cans were strewn all over and there were the remnants of charred stones in the shape of a firepit. Cardboard trays of takeaway food and crisp packets were blowing in the breeze. Cigarette butts lay discarded in the dirt. There were old car tyres and plastic canisters, which had been thrown over the fence. Inga could make out the wheel of an old bike rusting away in one of the bushes and a trainer was hanging from one of the branches in a tree.

The rest of the garden was so overgrown that she could hardly make out the bottom, all she could hear was the thundering sound of water from the stream behind the fence. The oak and hazel trees were covered in ivy and moss. Leaves were decaying on the floor. There were brambles growing uncontrollably over the wilted nettles. It smelled earthy, musky and damp and the ground underneath her feet was squelching with stagnant water. Branches of trees, broken off by the wind in the last big storm were blocking the path to what looked to be a shed. One branch had crashed through the roof and the window was hanging askew from its hinges. The door was ajar and creaking in the wind. The greenhouse at the side of the shed had been used for target practice and glass covered the floor. The place felt eerie. The trees stretched their bare branches like fingers devoid of flesh against the laden sky.

Standing in the mud, the fine rain covering her face, she felt uneasy and somehow watched. It felt like being in a graveyard and she expected for Gregory Peck to come through the gate looking for the secret that was buried underneath the slab in *The Omen*. She looked up and spotted a raven on a branch looking at her with its shiny black eyes. He let out a spine-chilling caw. Inga turned on her heels and fled, heart racing. She kicked the seating away from the gate, stepped through and locked it with cold and trembling fingers. Going home, Inga thought that she didn't like the place very much.

The next day, after yet another rain shower, the clouds parted and let the sun shine through. Armed with a saw, spade, dustpan and brush, she worked her way through the rubble. After she gathered all the rubbish and taken the car seat to the tip, she started to cut back the branches and dig out the weeds. She got up early and went home late. It carried on for weeks. Her husband sometimes helped on the weekend and the dog enjoyed sniffing in the dirt. On one of these occasions he found a dead pigeon and laid it at her feet like good retrievers do. They cleared the path all the way down to the old shed. She was looking forward to demolishing it. It would be fun as her next project. Inga was going to build a bigger one in its place.

Satisfied with her work she looked at the pile of wood in front of her. Taking the remnants of the shed up the path and lifting it into the van would be much harder. It took hours, walking up the path with a heavy load, conscious of the weight on her freshly healed leg, it was making her sweat. She had to rest and often catch her breath. She was no spring chicken any more and her back would not thank her in the morning. When she finished, she shut the door to the hire van and took one last look over her handiwork. The light was fading but she could make out an unusual dip in the square where she demolished the shed a few hours earlier. She walked back down some of the steps of the path that led to the bottom and took a closer look.

'I needed a pee, desperately, and it was getting dark, so it could have been a trick of the light,' she told her husband that evening. 'I thought it looked like the shape of a body.'

He dismissed it instantly, laughing.

'It wasn't funny, Jonathan,' she said and gave him the finger. 'I was scared and nearly peed myself. Stop laughing.'

'It's all those films you watch and the books you read while I am at work,' he said and she looked at him hurt.

'Because I'm doing nothing all day? Is that what you're saying?' Jonathan knew when to 'put the shovel down' as she called it, her own interpretation of 'If you're in a hole stop digging'.

'No, I'm saying that your imagination is running away with you. Tomorrow in the daylight it will look completely different DI Tennison.'

In the morning she returned to the plot and walked all the way down to where the shed had been. It had rained overnight and she could clearly see a rectangle in the square of the foundations. There was a shape of what she thought could be shoulders and collarbone at the top of the rectangle. Inga freaked out, imagining a headless corpse in the ground in front of her, she shuddered and dialled 999 for the police.

2.

Inga sat back in her car. The chap on the phone told her not to touch anything. 'A bit late for that,' she said to herself. She thought about all the potential evidence she may have destroyed over the last few weeks as she waited impatiently for the arrival of the police. She was itching to announce her find on Facebook.

She hadn't been that excited, since she was called for jury duty at Manchester Crown Court. She'd never surrendered her German passport but was honoured to perform her civic duty as an honorary British citizen. She felt important, having been chosen to be involved in such a far-reaching decision over somebody's life. She hoped it would be a case of murder and she was going to be the star of her own version of *Twelve Angry Men*. However, within two days her case was over. The evidence against the defendant was incriminating and captured on CCTV. The deliberation took almost half an hour and all the jury came to the same conclusion.

Excited, yet apprehensive, she looked out of the window, tapping her fingers on top of the steering wheel. Twenty minutes later she saw a police car in her rear-view mirror, driving down the muddy path.

'Hello,' the driver said, introducing himself as PC Mark Wilson. 'Are you the lady who reported a body in her garden?' He looked her up and down as if to get the full measure of a woman in charge of all her faculties. Inga chose to ignore his look and told the police officer what she had noticed. The policeman wrote it down in his little notebook.

'PC Wilson, can I call you Mark? While I sat in my car waiting for your arrival I thought about that missing man. Do you remember? Brian, something or the other. He was reported missing by his wife years ago. I moved into my house in 2003 so it must have been before that. He only lived down the road from here. At first, they believed that he had left the country but a few years later... I think it might have been 2004 because

I had to walk past the house for days on my way to work, the police searched her house and garden with scanning equipment. It was all a bit unsettling at the time, you know. To think somebody might have been murdered only a few doors down the road.' She stopped and shuddered.

'Do you know if he's ever been found?'

PC Wilson looked at her for a long moment.

'Can you take me down to the place where you think a body might be buried, Mrs Montgomery?' he asked, and she led him down the steps. He looked at the square piece of earth for a while, walking along the edges.

'I think I'm going to call the professionals and let them deal with this, Mrs Montgomery. Better not to compromise the soil. If you can wait at the top for now. I'll call this in.' He reached for his radio and started talking into it whilst following her up the steps.

Half an hour later a forensic van arrived and parked behind the police car. The policeman got out of his car and greeted the two colleagues. Inga stepped out of her car too. She waved at the group for their attention.

'PC Wilson, PC Wilson!' she shouted. 'Do you need me to do anything?'

PC Wilson shook his head and told her to go home, but she politely declined and sat back in her car. There was a knock on the side of her window which made her jump. Looking at the person she opened the door and stepped out onto the path.

'I'm Peter Graham. I have the plot next to yours,' he introduced himself, holding out his hand. She took it and shook it with enthusiasm.

'Nice to meet you, Peter, I'm Inga.'

'What happened?' he asked, offering her a drink from a flask. She repeated what she had told the police officer.

'It's not every day I'm in the middle of a real-life crime,' she said to Peter, who pulled a Blue Ribband biscuit out of his pocket and handed it to her.

'I should probably go home and make cups of tea for the guys. I probably have some cake as well.'

Leaning against the bonnet of her Mini, sheltering under a big umbrella because it had started to rain again, the two of them watched as a tent was erected over the spot where the shed used to be. The two people

23

in forensic white suits were getting ready to proceed. They had carefully removed a contraption from the back of their van which could only be described as a lawnmower on big wheels with a monitor on top of the handle.

'Mark,' Inga approached PC Wilson. 'Are you allowed to tell me what that machine does?'

'This machine, Mrs Montgomery, is the latest technology. It uses ground-penetrating radar to detect hidden objects. A bit like the X-ray machine at the airport.'

They watched over PC Wilson's shoulder as the team carefully carried the machine to the bottom. Not very unlike mowing the lawn they rolled the machine over the foundations of the shed, taking their time when pushing it over the rectangle. Then, suddenly, they stopped.

'Oh my God, Pete, they found something.' She grabbed hold of her neighbour's elbow to steady herself. Her mouth went dry and she took a sip from the mug. She didn't realise that her coffee had gone cold. Her palms felt sweaty and she hardly managed to stand still.

'Inga, stop getting so excited, you will give yourself a heart attack at this rate. Breathe!'

She was hopping from one leg to the other wringing her hands, mumbling, 'Oh my God, oh my God, oh my God. This is going to be big, huge, nothing like that ever happens to me, Pete! I'm just good old Inga, housewife, mother and Nana. I never even won big in the lottery.'

She handed the cup to him, edging herself closer through the gate for a better view. They waited with bated breaths.

One of the forensic officers pulled the mask off his face, shouted and gestured to his colleague, who handed him a spade. Minutes later they pulled what looked like a black plastic bag from the earth. Even from the distance and covered in mud it appeared to be one of those suit protector bags. They laid it on the floor. One of the officers felt the bag from the outside and sent what looked like a torch inside the bag. They looked at the monitor and then in her direction, shaking their heads. This didn't look good.

'I'm ever so sorry, Officer,' she said again, red faced and flushed with embarrassment as PC Wilson walked towards her carrying the dirty bag over his arm.

'It really looked like there was a body buried there and with the man still missing I thought, well, I thought....' She looked past PC Wilson where she could see one of the forensic officers stepping out of his white suit. The other one was already packing up the tent, probably cursing her under his breath for having to carry the heavy machine back up the path.

PC Wilson handed the bag to her.

'There was nothing in the earth apart from this suit, Mrs Montgomery. We are one hundred percent certain that no crime has been committed here. Therefore, we are not going to take this bag into evidence and you can keep it as a memento, if you want,' he said and walked back to his car, making some more notes in his little book.

How embarrassing. She threw the bag into the boot of her car and said goodbye to Peter. After a long wait for the police to move their equipment back into the van and more pitiful looks by the forensic team, which brought tears to her eyes, she locked the gate and headed home. Still feeling deflated and humiliated she opened the door. Even the sight of Toby, who greeted her with a wagging tale and the enthusiasm only dogs have when they have been left for a while, couldn't cheer her up.

'Thankfully I didn't put in on Facebook,' she said to her husband later that night and felt another wave of heat creeping into her cheeks.

'That is so typical of me. I'm so embarrassed.'

'Very typical. Come here, babe.' He held his arms out and she walked into his embrace. She couldn't see his lips curling upwards at the sides. 'Never mind, hey? Just be grateful that it wasn't a body after all. Nobody will know. Don't worry about it.'

That night she didn't get much sleep. The events of the day were still going around in her head. She hoped she'd got away with her little disaster. Nobody noticed the police vans on her plot other than her neighbour, who she'd sworn to secrecy. She just couldn't shake the feeling of embarrassment.

The next morning Inga fetched the dirty bag from the boot of her car and was in the middle of cleaning it when the telephone rang. She wiped her hands and picked up the phone. It was her best friend Liberty.

'Hi, hon, you made the papers.'

Libby was her oldest and closest friend. She was the opposite of Inga. Libby would look good in a black binbag. She had all the right curves in the right places and considered surgery and Botox a necessity. Inga, having rediscovered a taste for baking, combined with the overindulgence of her new favourite drink, rhubarb gin, chocolate, soda bread and butter, didn't have curves, she had a chassis. Inga compared Libby to a Porsche. Stylish, elegant, expensive. Inga had turned into a Volvo, comfortable, reliable, sturdy. It didn't matter what time Inga arrived at Libby's house, she was always immaculate, make-up, hair, nails. Inga didn't quite care most days, no make-up, hair in a bun (there was no way she would spend hours to straighten it), short and practical nails. Libby was confident, vibrant and normally got what she wanted. Inga, not so much.

They had known each other since forever. Their sons used to play rugby at the same club and were best friends. Their husbands like brothers. They'd been on shared holidays together and had the same sense of humour. It didn't matter what time Inga rang Libby. Even in the middle of the night she would listen to her rants about the kids, husband and co-workers. She had solved more than one problem for Inga over the years.

'Shit,' Inga replied. 'You are taking the piss. Was it in yesterday's paper? They didn't print my name, did they? What does it say?'

Libby read the article back to her. All of a sudden it became clear why the people on the bridle path this morning smiled at her knowingly.

'That must have been really exciting. What was in the bag?'

'They printed my name?' Inga was mortified. 'I haven't opened it yet.' She could see Libby rolling her eyes through the phone.

'Come on. Are you not in the least curious?'

'I am, I was in the middle of cleaning the bag when you rang. Can you imagine how embarrassed I was when they found it? I feel quite sick now.'

'Why?' Libby replied. 'It's not like anybody else ever made a mistake like that.'

Inga wasn't so sure. 'It will be something utterly unimportant and ordinary anyway,' she said deflated.

'Open it, you silly mare, and let me know what's in it. Speak to you later, babe. Love you.' And with that she ended her call.

Inga sighed, boiled the kettle for another cup of coffee and continued scrubbing the rust off the zip with a wire brush. When she finished she laid the bag out on the kitchen table to dry. There it remained till her husband arrived home. He entered the kitchen, where she was cooking dinner.

'Hi, babe.' He tried not to trip over the dog, who was expectantly wagging his tail, barking for the treat he deserved for looking after his mum all day.

'Why on earth is this in here?' He pointed at the table, bending down and stroking the dog behind its ears.

'I would have thought you'd had a peek by now. The suspense must be killing you.' He smiled and kissed her on the neck. She nudged him with her elbow.

'I didn't want to open it without you. It might be crawling with spiders.' She imagined hundreds of spiders, crawling out of the bag all over her kitchen table, and shuddered.

'It's got a zip that has been fastened shut by rust and it was buried under a shed,' he said. 'There won't be any creatures inside.'

She reminded him of the mouse infestation they had over the winter. 'They didn't have an obvious entrance to our extension but still managed to get in. Eleven mice,' she recalled. 'Eleven, Jon.' What a mess that had been. He lifted the bag off the table and let it drop to the floor.

'I'm starving, can we eat first?'

After they loaded the dishwasher he lifted the bag off the floor and placed it back on the table. He struggled with the zip but with a little oil managed to open it in the end. He put his hand into the bag and felt for a hanger but there wasn't one. As he laid the jacket out on the table they both looked at each other.

The jacket was green, it had probably been a dark olive colour when it was new. They turned it around to study it closer. On its right sleeve was a badge. It was made from two squares that were placed at an angle which made the outer shape into a star. It was green in colour with a blue outer circle. A red circle in the middle was framed by a golden triangle. On those circles they could see writing in, what she presumed, was Arabic. There was a red triangle sewn right above the badge and a gold eagle on each shoulder strap. Brownish splatters were visible all over the

27

front of the jacket. He lifted the flap on the right breast pocket and felt the inside. His fingers touched a piece of paper, carefully prising it loose, he slid it out. The paper was folded and brittle, the writing yellow and faded.

'What is it?' she asked her husband who had stepped back from the table, note in hand. He shook his head in disbelief, turning the piece of paper in his hands, looking from one to the other.

'This looks like a page from a newspaper and that, my darling,' he pointed to the uniform, 'is an Iraqi Republican Guard uniform.'

Inga looked at him frowning and cautiously stepped towards the uniform as if it was carrying a terrible disease within. She pulled up a chair and sat down.

3.

The man suddenly woke from his dream. He had a little difficulty letting go of the face he saw in his nightmare.

'You killed me.' The sentence still hangs in the air. His heart was racing and his pyjama top felt damp with sweat. He looked over to his sleeping wife and, so not to disturb her, got out of bed and walked into the kitchen. Sitting down at the table he looked at his shaking hands. He thought he had buried the secret along with the uniform but reading the paper today brought it all back. He should have burnt the damned thing but he could not part with it.

He felt something behind his back. There was a touch as light as a feather on his neck. He imagined the dead man's hands on his neck, closing his fingers around his throat and closed his eyes. He held his breath in anticipation of the choke.

'Can't you sleep, my darling?' his wife whispered in his ear. 'I woke up and you weren't there. You have been distant all day. What is troubling you?' She put her arms around his neck.

'Come on, come back to bed.'

Recognising her voice, he swirled her around and sat her across his lap, pulling her into an embrace. Relieved, he inhaled her sweet scent. Breathing more easily and feeling her warm breath on the side of his neck he thought that everything was all right. It was just a dream. Nobody was coming for him.

'You go ahead, I will be right behind you.' She kissed him gently on his lips. 'Don't be long,' she said. 'I'm cold.'

As she lay in her bed, trying to go back to sleep, she thought of their lives together. His love for her had kept her alive. They arrived in the UK in 1991 and their application for asylum had been granted a year later.

They moved from London to the north of England where he bought a small greengrocers' shop and they lived in the apartment above. She didn't know where the money had come from but hadn't asked. They weren't well off, but she didn't want for anything. It was as if he could read her mind. But still there was something missing which would have made their lives complete. If only she could have given him children. They had tried but had never been blessed. Now as they were getting older, she wondered if this was the reason he couldn't sleep. Who would look after them when he was too old to work? Moments later she heard the door open quietly. He got into bed and nestled himself into her back. He put an arm protectively around her and kissed the back of her neck.

'I love you,' he whispered but she didn't hear him. She had already drifted back off to sleep.

4.

It had been four months since Jonathan sat with his family around the table on holiday with his in-laws. They were laughing and joking when a news bulletin flashed onto the TV screen. Saddam Hussein and his Iraqi Republican Army had invaded Kuwait. They all sat in silence.

'Well,' his father-in-law said. 'We saw that coming, didn't we, Klaudia?' he said to his wife. His father-in-law was very knowledgeable when it came to politics, Inga had told him, and Jonathan had no doubt that if he could speak German fluently, he would've had to discuss these kinds of topics every time they visited her parents. There were small mercies after all.

'It's common knowledge that the Iraqi president is at war with the West,' his father-in-law continued. 'Saddam is bankrupt. His country accumulated a huge debt in fighting against Khomeini. Eight years of war resulting in the loss of millions of lives does that to a country, we should know.' His mother-in-law nodded her head in agreement. 'The revolt in the Kurdish north of the country that he brutally quashed with a gas attack on Halabja. How can any government carry on talking to a man who has no scruples in killing his own people?' His father-in-law shook his head. 'Madness, utter madness.' His father-in-law looked at Jonathan as if he could understand a single word and continued.

'Kuwait supported Iraq during the war against Iran and are now demanding repayment but undercutting the oil prices? It's no wonder he's furious and feels abandoned. However, Kuwait gained independence by the British government after the First World War and just can't be invaded like that. It's not part of Iraq any more. It's an act of war.' He poured more red wine and sat back.

His father-in-law was on a roll. 'If you ask me, Saddam saw an opportunity to get rid of his debt and absorb Kuwait back into his territory. He clearly doesn't care what the rest of the world thinks.'

'This is going to be my next deployment,' Jonathan said to his wife jokingly at the time. Inga translated what he said and everybody at the table looked at him in shock.

His tour of duty to Northern Ireland still fresh on his wife's mind, she looked at him in despair. By the time they returned from their holidays the United Nations Security Council had condemned the invasion.

'Passing resolution which requests, REQUESTS the withdrawal from Kuwait. Who politely requests a withdrawal when your country has forcefully been invaded?' he had said to his wife many times.

'They have to try and resolve this peacefully, don't you think?' his wife replied forever hopeful and she was devastated when another resolution in November was passed which authorized the use of force against the Iraqi occupation. Jonathan had a different opinion but he kept that to himself because he knew better than to rock the boat. He knew that the United States of America were already on operation in the Gulf area. Forces from thirty-four other countries, including Britain were being made ready to join them. The deadline was set for the 15th of January.

Every day Jonathan came home she had the same question for him and for a week he told her that the army were only looking to find volunteers.

'You are not going to volunteer for this, Jonathan. I forbid it. Don't you dare step forward and get involved in this shit. Why would you voluntarily go out to be shot at? Let the unmarried soldiers go and support the American units if they want.' At the time he thought that she was being very selfish since those soldiers had families too, but he also kept that thought to himself. He would have volunteered in a jiffy.

The decision about volunteering was soon taken away from him since it became clear that the British Army was going to send a much bigger force than first anticipated. He was in the REME and the whole workshop was being made ready to go. He struggled to explain to his wife that as a soldier it was his job. He signed a contract to fight for Queen and Country and he was proud to honour that promise.

'They've given us three weeks' leave, love,' he said to her after he came back from another exercise.

'Three weeks? Wow, that's very kind of them. Three weeks,' she said sarcastically and burst out crying. He felt terrible for her but couldn't understand why she was getting upset about something that hadn't even happened yet. Yes, he could die but he wasn't going to and he was part of the biggest military operation since World War Two and proud of it. He spent the last three weeks in December saying his goodbyes to family and friends in England and left for Saudi Arabia the day after New Year.

They were put onto planes at RAF Gütersloh and after hours of uncomfortable flying landed on an airstrip near Riyadh in Saudi Arabia. He looked at his comrades. Like his, their eyes were blurry and red. They were tired and sweaty. Unlike normal planes there was no on-board entertainment and no trolley dollies looked after them with complimentary drinks and snacks. At least they had a seat and he tried to get some sleep. Regardless of the noise of the engine he had put his head against the seat in front of him and nodded off. Soldiers were taught to sleep anywhere. No fanfare sounded and nobody applauded the pilot for arriving on time and landing safely. When he stepped through the door the heat took the air out of his lungs. Like jumping into cold water only the other way around. He was reminded of stepping into a sauna and the hot air burnt in the back of his throat. He took shallow gulps of breath till he got used to the heat. He was under no illusion that it was going to get hotter as the day went by.

They collected their belongings and were issued with guns, 9mm SMGs on arrival, waiting again to be loaded onto Stagecoach double-decker buses that had been shipped in from Britain.

He passed a board on the back of the coach he was going to travel on. It was advertising a show in the Alhambra Theatre in Bradford. When he sat down he read the graffiti on the side of the walls. 'Amy was here' it read. 'Sue loves Bradley' and I 'heart' Bradford. He found it bizarre to find the name of his home town on a coach that was thousands of miles away. Being on it felt weird. As if he was taking a bus into town on a normal day. He wondered if Amy, Sue or Bradley had chewed the gum he saw stuck on the headrest in front of him. Did he know Amy? Did Bradley have a job? Did Sue care that they were going to war or was she asleep in bed with Bradley after having had great sex? Looking at the chewing gum, carelessly discarded in front of him, he thought probably not. He looked at his watch and thought of his little family back home, wondering what they were doing at that moment in time.

Hungry and tired they arrived at the port of Al Jubail after an endless drive through the Saudi desert. There was nothing much to see or do on the journey. They passed sand dune after sand dune along the road, palm trees were surrounding the occasional dwelling. Inexplicably the camels standing at the side of the road reminded him of the sheep he passed in his car on the Yorkshire Moors.

'You couldn't run one of these over and stick it in the boot, could you?' he said to the soldier sitting next to him and they laughed.

'I think the car would be a write-off, mate,' the soldier replied and they both sank back into their seats, each of them left to their own thoughts.

He wanted to be a soldier all his life. His mother wasn't impressed when he dug trenches in her garden as a child and used the flowerbeds as cover against an imaginary enemy. He would run around shooting his toy gun pretending to be John Wayne, shouting 'Take that you scumbags.' When he was a little older and his mum allowed him to watch films about the Vietnam war, *Apocalypse Now* became his favourite film and he wished he could have been there. In 1982 he was too young when Britain went to war with Argentina over the Falkland Islands but he collected all the magazines he could find about the conflict. He knew exactly why he wanted to join the forces. He wanted to be a hero.

He'd always been a loveable 'rogue'. Charismatic and charming, standing up for the bullied kid at school by beating his tormentors, but equally happy to participate in fighting pupils from a rivals school after lessons. He played rugby at school and at club level and his position was at prop. He was the 'Enforcer'. His short temper and willingness to participate in fights had earned him the name 'Pitbull' on and off the pitch. He wasn't going out of his way looking for trouble but trouble often found him. Growing up in the eighties wasn't for wimps.

He asked for permission from his parents to join the army at sixteen but his mother refused point blank. He was determined and one day decided to run away with his best friend Mark to join the French Foreign Legion. They boarded the train to go to London but Mark changed his mind halfway through. His mother never found out.

When he was eighteen he didn't need his parents' permission and visited the recruitment office for the Marines in Leeds. 'I want to join the Marines,' he said to the chap, hobbling along on crutches with his leg in plaster after a car accident. He was fuming that they refused him because of his broken leg. He tried again a year later at the Army Careers office in Bradford and they signed him up to become a vehicle mechanic. He went home and told his father first.

It had become very hot on the coach, there was no air conditioning, not even blinds to shelter them from the blazing sun. He liked it hot on his holidays but this was taking the piss. They passed through the gates of the camp made from shipping containers stacked two to three high and found their accommodation. Portakabins had been shipped in and were dotted around the complex. These also had no air conditioning. They walked passed the Land Rovers, Bedford trucks and armoured vehicles to their hut. Inside there were shelves for their belongings and a fold-up camp bed too small for a comfortable night's sleep, no luxuries like a mattress or sheets. They were issued sleeping bags and collected their desert combats, boots and NBC kits (nuclear, biological and chemical kits). When they dropped their desert kit on their cots, there was a buzz about the group of men he served with. They were all excited about the prospect of a real battle ahead of them. They were briefed later that afternoon and even though they didn't know what to expect, having been warned about the strength of the Republican Guard and the threat of chemical weapons, they were confident that this war wasn't going to last long. The firepower of the NATO allies was far superior to anything Saddam could throw at them. They were working twelve-hour shifts and exhausted, hardly able to find time to write home. They were given telephone cards to ring home from the phones in camp but he couldn't cram anything he wanted to say into five minutes. It was great to hear his wife's voice on the other end of the phone but time was never enough and soldiers were waiting impatiently behind him, tapping him on the shoulder to finish.

Because of a very real threat of the use of Weapons of Mass Destruction (WMDs) by Saddam, the army had given orders that every soldier would have to be treated with an injection of an untrialled anthrax and bubonic plague vaccine. They were also given NAPS tablets (Nerve

Agent Pre-treatment Systems). He felt a little bit like a guinea pig. Standing in line with everybody else, he received his injections and swallowed the tablets. Continuing his work, he passed out trying to push-start a Land Rover. He had been bedded down for twenty-four hours but was deployed from Al Jubail to a location only identifiable by a grid reference in the desert a week later.

There they waited for the tanks to arrive. The Challenger tanks had to be fitted with additional armour for protection before being sent to the front line. His arm, which had received the injection, swelled up and he had to visit a field hospital two miles away. The infected boil was lanced. Two years later, they would remove the tiny tip of the needle which had broken off still festering in his arm. The deadline of the ultimatum for the Iraqis to leave Kuwait had come and gone and two days later they could hear the B52 bombers flying over their heads into the distance to release their deadly cargo onto Baghdad and Kuwait. The planes flew mostly at night and the soldiers got used to the deep humming sound above their heads. They waited impatiently for the ground offensive to begin.

A few weeks after the first bombers flew over their heads, they were suddenly woken in the middle of the night by an almighty bang in the distance. Everyone on Jonathan's crew was asleep on top of their tank. They jumped up and scrambled to the ground, guns at the ready, squinting into the night looking for the enemy. Even if they would have been issued with radio equipment, they didn't have the same frequency as the Americans and consequently were unaware that an American MRLS (Multiple Rocket Launch System) had taken up position in the night just two kilometres away. Missiles were being fired over their heads. They watched in awe as none of them had witnessed anything like it before.

The noise was deafening even at that distance and their eyes followed the glow of the afterburn of the rockets being fired onto enemy positions miles in front of them. It was exhilarating and frightening at the same time. They were high fiving and shouting at one another over the noise. He suddenly had to think of his grandad who witnessed the aftermath of the D-Day landings and the horror at the concentration camp at Bergen-Belsen. Unfortunately, his grandad died shortly before he was born of a massive brain haemorrhage. Jonathan would've loved to have talked to him about the War.

'Your grandfather didn't often talk about it,' his mother said when he pestered her again about his grandad and the War and, on one occasion, she recalled his favourite saying.

'When the Germans fired, the British ducked and when the British fired, the Germans ducked. When the Americans fired, everybody ducked.' He chuckled as he recalled the conversation. Jonathan didn't care who fired. Finally, the wait was over. The battle he signed up for was going to be fought and he was going to be part of it.

5.

The girl sat on the sand and looked out across the water. The sun was rising above the top of the hills and she felt almost safe. She walked hundreds of miles through the dirt to get to where the boats were waiting. She had endured starvation and thirst, dragging her body ever forward in the hope that she would survive. She had made it, avoided rape and capture by sex traffickers by tagging along with various families. It didn't make her trip safe, she saw girls and boys being abducted even with their families nearby; however it was better than travelling alone. She hid from thieves who would steal anything of value from the ragged people travelling on the road. She had managed to pay for her crossing. She had been lucky.

Covered by a heavy sheet of plastic, stuffed together like sardines they had left the coast of Turkey the night before. It had been a rough crossing. The small boat, overloaded with people, was violently thrown from side to side. She saw two people lose their balance. They were thrown overboard by a wave crashing against the side of the boat. Nobody bothered throwing them a rope. She hoped that they were lucky and wearing a life jacket but there hadn't been one for everybody when she got on board. Their bodies were washed out to sea, their screams for help drowned out by the wind. She held hands with the woman next to her. Their fingers fused together by the cold wet water. At some point in the night they were given plastic cups to scoop the rising water into buckets from the bottom of the boat. She was grateful to escape the stench of fear, lifting her head from under the plastic cover, breathing fresh air, pouring the water over the side. That night she thought she was going to die.

When the front of the boat scraped over the sand of the beach in the morning she said a quick prayer to Allah to thank him for his mercy. A nice woman helped her escape the belly of the boat and put her on the sand. She gave her a bottle of water and an apple she pulled from her pocket. The girl looked around and saw a hotel at the far side of the beach. A dog with three legs was hopping towards her from underneath an olive tree looking at her with curious eyes. Exhausted, feeling the warming sun on her face, the girl started to feel hopeful at last. 'I will just sit here and close my eyes for a second.' And with that she fell asleep. The dog sat next to her and watched as many more people were lifted onto the beach.

6.

Inga looked at the uniform in front of her and tried to digest the words her husband had just spoken. She felt sick to her stomach. All the forgotten memories and emotions suddenly came rushing back. She felt faint.

'Can I have a drink?' she asked her husband. He handed her a glass of water. She had become good at compartmentalising and all the bad stuff should have been stored away and buried. She never wanted to think about that time again. It was supposed to be in the past. But here it was. She was staring at it. An undeniable item of the darkest days of her life.

She met her husband in a student bar in January 1988. The gods of love must have been very bored that night because they should never have met. She used to hang out with a lot of English students from the polytechnic in Hull. Sonya was teaching Inga to speak better English and she was teaching Sonya German in return. On that fateful night Inga reluctantly agreed to go out for a birthday party in the 'Tenner Bar'. Her future husband travelled down from Minden to visit an army friend. This friend however was on duty that night so he should have driven back to his barracks, instead he stayed and went out to the same bar for a drink. With every beer Inga's English was getting better so that by the end of the night she was almost fluent. He mistook her for one of the English students and asked her for a dance. She gave him her number and he rang a few days later. English was never her forte in school but they hit it off despite of the language barrier. He put it down to the universal language of love. She introduced him to her parents who said they liked him but couldn't hold a conversation unless she translated. Inga fell pregnant during an alcohol-infused Easter weekend at her parents' house. He had gone on tour to Northern Ireland two weeks later, unaware.

She was frightened and didn't think she would hear from him again when she told him of the baby on the phone as the line went dead. Luckily, he rang straight back and reassured her that everything was going to be fine. Inga visited his parents on his R&R halfway through his six-month tour. He told his mother that she was pregnant on the day he went back to Belfast and a letter from his mother arrived at Inga's house a week later telling her she would ruin her son's life. Despite all this the baby was born in December and they were married in February 1989 in a German registry office. His parents didn't attend through work commitments. Her father was absent. They had been married nearly thirty years and her mother-in-law loved her like the daughter she never had.

Nobody could have prepared her for married life in the army. Her identity as an individual person vanished. She was now known as the 'wife of' her husband's rank and number. Many women she felt were wearing their husbands' rank like badges of honour. The higher the rank of her husband the higher the status a wife thought she had. It was a little bizarre and it took her a while to get used to. She learned not to shout at an ASM (Artificer Sergeant Major) for putting her husband down in public, learned that ironing two creases in his army trousers, shrinking his woollen jumper in the wash or giving him the wrong haircut would get him weekend duties or worse a day in jail. She was given an ID card and had to take a driving test even though she was in possession of a German driving licence. It had been a steep learning curve. There were new rules and regulations but she was with the man she loved. He just happened to be a soldier in the British Army.

The day after they got married, she moved from her home town to his barracks in Minden, three and a half hours away from her parents. It was hard being on her own with a newborn baby, far away from the support of her family and friends. She felt isolated at the beginning since he was either on exercise or at a rugby game. She spent a lot of time driving down the motorway in her first year of marriage. He was posted to Münster the following year and they had been allocated a lovely ground-floor flat with a balcony overlooking a playground. The block was surrounded by trees and there was a beautiful castle nearby, inviting them on Sunday walks. There were German shops in the village and a NAAFI nearby. Then Iraq invaded Kuwait and everything changed.

She was so angry with him when he came home to tell her the news that the whole of his workshop was being made ready to go. First, she was quietly devastated, then she shouted and screamed.

'Why can they not send someone else instead of you?' she ranted. 'I am too young to become a widow. You could just refuse to go! Nobody is going to stand you in front of a firing squad any more.'

She didn't understand why the British Government had to get involved in a war that wasn't theirs, let the Arabs sort themselves out.

'I have signed the dotted line,' he usually replied. 'It's my job after all.' It had infuriated her even more.

She would probably have been protesting with the German peace movement as she was a peaceful person, but now she shook her head at them lying on the floor. They wouldn't change anything. What was the point? Their husbands and brothers weren't made to go to war. She was angry when she overheard the English wives talking behind her back, condemning the Germans for not contributing to the war like everyone else. Did they know that the German constitution forbade Germany to ever pick up arms again after World War Two? She was stuck in the middle.

Sadness followed rage, rage was followed by hopefulness of a last-minute peaceful resolution. In the end, she had to resign herself to the fact that there was nothing anybody, neither government nor God would do, to prevent this war.

7.

He left them the day after New Year. Inga and her daughter waved goodbye to her husband and the other soldiers on the coaches not knowing whether they would ever see him again. The tears she cried that day. Christmas and New Year had never been the same since. The song *Mother's Pride* by George Michael was released just before Christmas that year and hearing it on the radio still reduced her to tears years later. Inga saw herself, clutching her child, standing at an open coffin looking down on her husband's lifeless body. Would she have to tell their daughter that he lost his life fighting for Queen and Country in a senseless war or that he died a hero?

There were no mobile phones or e-mails in those days and they kept in touch through blueys. These were blue-coloured letters that folded in on themselves containing messages of eternal love and happiness. These were good for morale the women were told, they should be full of cheer and bliss. Inga had to go out and collect the mail every couple of days from the family's office. Most days there was no letter waiting and she was devastated, always thinking the worst. When one did arrive, the joy was endless. However, the letters were always days behind.

For obvious reasons the men were not allowed to say anything that would compromise the mission or give information that could upset the women at home. Consequently, her letters were long about their everyday life and his letters were short and about how much he missed them. There was an occasional phone call at the beginning when he still had access to a phone but, after a while, she had to stop sitting near the phone just on the off chance he was going to ring. Life went on. The family office was there to support the women left behind and they would arrange meetings like coffee mornings, meals and days out for the families. However, she didn't live in close proximity of the camp, and since she didn't belong to a regiment as such, those occasions were rare.

A lot of the women went home to be with their parents. Inga mostly kept herself to herself. There were good times and bad. The women pulled together in the face of adversity. However, there were also women who spread malicious rumours. Inga suspected that it happened because they were bored. She remembered one of her neighbours had seen a German man arriving at Inga's door. The man was Inga's brother but her neighbour suspected her of having an affair and told everyone who cared to listen. Inga didn't want to be a part of that so she spent the weekends with her family.

The TV was the only accurate source of information it seemed. With hindsight she should have ripped the cable out of the wall.

Even though she knew that her husband wasn't involved in the first four weeks of the war she was glued to the television 24/7. She remembered the sickening feeling in her stomach the minute she opened her eyes to the moment she fell asleep, the images of the air assault on Baghdad still flashing on her TV screen. She felt despair when Saddam launched Scud missiles into Israel, provoking them to retaliate and start an all-out war with the Muslim states in the region. Thankfully nobody was injured and the glorified Patriot missile did its job in intercepting the Scuds, rendering them useless. The threat of chemical attacks remained.

She was frightened to death when the ground war was finally announced on the television. Till that point she was still hopeful that Saddam would leave Kuwait of his own accord. He would be mad to think that he could win this war. She would never forget the war correspondent Kate Adie reporting from the front line. Tank after tank, moving forward in unison towards the battlefield, leaving dust clouds behind, the British flag blowing in the wind. If she didn't know what was about to happen it would have looked awesome, but because she did it was terrifying.

She was furious when they reported the death of nine soldiers from American 'friendly fire'. She cried when she saw the coffins, draped in the British flag being carried slowly from the plane, arriving at RAF Brize Norton to be repatriated. Nine hearses waiting in line on the tarmac, each of them driving forward to receive a loved one, watched by their wives, children, fathers and mothers, sisters and brothers. Tears were streaming down her face, seeing the black funeral cars making their way slowly through Carterton village near Brize Norton Air Base. People, some standing quietly at the side of the road, throwing flowers on the bonnets in passing, others clapping in recognition of what those soldiers had sacrificed for their country. It would stay with her forever. She was equally shocked by the pictures hundreds of burnt-out vehicles on the road to Basra. Hundreds of people had died. Such an unnecessary waste of lives.

Inga lived in constant fear that one day somebody would knock on her door and her heart jumped into her throat every time an unknown car pulled up outside her block of flats. Many times, she cried herself to sleep with her child wrapped closely in her arms. At the end of the six weeks she was a shadow of her former self.

Then the war was over. It was like having been woken from a long sleep where time stood still. But unlike Sleeping Beauty it was more like a nightmare that left a lingering sick feeling in her gut and was hard to shake off.

Instead of chasing Saddam back to Baghdad, like the dog he was with his tail between his legs, dealing with him the only way that seemed just, America declared a ceasefire. It was incomprehensible. Inga didn't understand how they could leave that evil man to continue his reign of terror. Was this war not going to be about his removal? Saddam was a monster and deserved to be captured and made held accountable. Was he supposed to live and continue the horror? Where was the justice in that? Exhausted and tired she packed up her daughter and travelled to England to be with his parents.

Through lack of support from the British government and nobody to speak to but Inga, her mother-in-law had formed her own support group. After a first big response from an advert she placed in the paper, the group ended up being rather small. Just three mothers with sons fighting in the Gulf. It was enough to help her mother-in-law through her darkest days. They organised parcels to be sent to the troops and they even made it into the local newspaper.

'We are now known as the page three girls you know,' one of them said with pride to Inga when they met her for a meal at the local Italian. Inga smiled at the thought, her mother-in-law's chest was nowhere near page three material, not even in her younger days. In the end there was nothing else left to do but to wait for news that Jonathan was coming home.

Now, Inga was staring at the uniform that evoked fear and sadness and she asked herself why somebody had hidden it under the shed.

8.

Hakim needed to get out and he had to find her. She was probably frightened and out of her mind. Since they invaded Kuwait in August things had gone from bad to worse. After seeing the fleeing Kuwaiti Army and the looting had stopped, the triumph had given way to uncertainty. The United Nations Security Council, by that he really meant the American infidels under the command of President George Bush, had given them till the 15th of January to retreat. Several attempts to negotiate a peaceful solution had come to nothing. Their great leader and President Saddam Hussein had insisted that his army could not be beaten on the battlefield. He had threatened to release chemical weapons in the event of interference by the West.

They rounded up the foreign civilian workers and their families, using them as human shields. The people were put under guard in strategic locations like Kuwait City Airport. He remembered the chemical attack in 1988 on the Kurdish population during the Iran war and was sure that the world had no doubt that Saddam wouldn't have any hesitation in releasing these gases a second time. Thousands died that day in 1988. Men, women and children. Young and old alike along with their livestock.

The world was outraged and the UN Security Council had condemned the invasion. They had authorised a task force, spearheaded by the American traitors, to drive them from the land that was theirs by right. Hakim had seen the reports for himself in their last meeting. Gunships arrived just of the coast of Kuwait and there had been sightings and repeated landings of amphibious assault vehicles. This was surely a diversion for the real attack. But he could not convince his commanders. Saddam was certain they could win an outright war because he simply wished it.

Hakim was fifteen but he remembered the day when Saddam showed his ruthlessness for the first time well. Sitting in front of the black and white television in 1979 with his best friend he watched a young

46

Saddam Hussein, who had just become their president, standing in a large auditorium filled with government officials. Saddam, solemn and composed, announced that he had uncovered a plot and brought out a sad and frightened-looking man who confessed to taking part in a conspiracy to overthrow the new government. He started calling out the traitors' names and nineteen men were escorted from the building. A hundred and forty-eight members of the Ba'ath party had been identified in all and would be executed. Hakim didn't know it then, but this event, and others that followed would be the main accusation in Saddam's trial of crimes against humanity and his subsequent execution.

In the year that followed Saddam Hussein ruled the country with an iron fist, the police were brutal and cruel. To hold down a job his father, like most people, had become a member of the nationalistic Pan-Arabic Ba'ath Party. His father was forced to attend more and more party meetings and the way to get ahead in the party was to become a 'follower'.

'We are encouraged to spy on our neighbours and friends, Hakim. This is not going to end well,' he said. 'How do you know if somebody is telling the truth or a lie? It's happening already. I've seen it at work. Mr Hammad told a joke about Saddam's moustache and the next day he was gone.' He fell silent.

'Be very mindful what you say at school, son. There are spies everywhere.' He still heard his father's voice when he took the bus to his new school. He looked around for the first time with his eyes wide open. Pictures of Saddam were on every street corner and every square. He was a hero, depicted riding on a white stallion, a man of the people, surrounded by children, a statesman in full tribal regalia, looking out for his people, holding children in his arms. Hakim asked himself how his father could be so frightened. How could he not trust a man who asked the children to call him 'Uncle'?

A year later, Hakim witnessed how his neighbour of many years was driven from his home. He was of Iranian descent, living in Iraq for generations but like all Iranians he was rounded up and expelled from the country of his birth. He watched as his neighbour was sent packing with just a few belongings he could carry and was marched to the end of the street escorted by armed soldiers. He heard rumours at school that the

47

women were raped and men beaten. If they survived and reached the safety on the other side of the border, they were held in camps, suspected of being Iraqi spies.

He was unable to help any of his friends who were rounded up by the new secret police force. The Mukhabarat's eyes and ears were everywhere. They arrested people at random, tortured and killed. He'd seen people being dragged from their homes and executed in the street. His teacher had been one of them. He heard that the men of the Mukhabarat videoed the rape of his wife and threatened to release the video if she didn't comply with spying on her husband. The teacher's wife didn't see another way but to end her life out of shame, her family unable to take her back because she'd been dishonoured. There were stories being told behind closed doors that her husband's body was returned without his head so his family was unable to bury him with dignity. Many men were sent to prison, tortured for making a remark about Saddam or Saddam's family. Those people were never heard of again.

Then the war with Iran started. Men who refused to join the army were sent to the front regardless, their families threatened with death. Rich families were more fortunate and sometimes able to buy their way out. Their sons were simply sent to foreign countries to study. Hakim dreaded the day he knew was inevitable and they would come for him. One day in 1981 his friend Amir received a letter, conscripting him into the army to fight the Iranians.

'I've made up my mind. I'm going to go with Amir, Father.' His father smiled, had taken him in his arms and hugged him tight.

'You don't need to go, son. You haven't had a letter yet. Saddam is frightened that the revolution of Ayatollah Khomeini's Iran is spilling over to the Shia population here. The war isn't as clear cut as Saddam expected it to be after the first year, son. He's ordering the men to pick up arms and defend our country. You are too young to fight, Hakim. You've not even finished your schooling yet.'

'Neither has Amir, Father. I can't let him go by himself. I promised. They'll come for me anyway, eventually.'

'Hakim, I've spoken to cousin Abas in Bagdad and he needs an aid. You don't need to go to war. I've arranged it so you can work with him in the government.' Hakim shook his head. 'You don't understand, *Baba*, I've promised Nazreen.'

'What's your obsession with that girl, Hakim? She's too young for you. The whole family isn't good for you. I've tolerated your friendship so far but you must stop this nonsense at once. You're my only son. What am I going to do without you?' Hakim straightened his back.

'Please don't speak of her like that, Father. I'm going with Amir. I've promised.' There were tears in his father's eyes and he turned his head towards the wall and motioned Hakim to leave the room. Hakim had never seen him cry before, not even at his mother's funeral and he left, shutting the door quietly behind him.

On the day they left, his and Amir's father stood side by side. Amir's mother was hovering behind her husband wiping her eyes and crying quietly into her sleeve. Nazreen was nowhere to be seen.

'Where is she, Amir? I need to say my goodbye to her. I can't leave without seeing her one more time.' He asked himself how she could be so cruel. Amir's father took him by the shoulders and kissed him on each cheek.

'Look after each other, Hakim. You're the older one and I'm relying on you to keep him safe. He's the only son I have left.'

Hakim looked at his father and they departed with a nod to each other. He had kissed his father earlier and promised to be careful. They walked slowly towards the end of the street where a bus would be waiting. Suddenly he heard his name being shouted from behind and Nazreen came running towards him. She flew into his arms and held him close.

'Bring it back to me,' she whispered in his ear and she slipped something in his coat pocket. Before he could say anything, she stepped back, hugged her brother and vanished between the houses. Hakim's fingers touched his pocket. He knew without looking that it was the stone he'd found at the river bank.

They were driven to a stretch of land in the desert where they were subjected to the gruelling regime of army life. In a very short time, they learned how to fire a gun, build defences, crawl under barbed wire and stab straw dummies with bayonets, all the while being shouted at by the instructors of the Republican Guard who stood behind them with batons in hand. After a few weeks, they were put back onto coaches covered in mud to distract any enemy fire and driven to where the fighting was fiercest. They weren't 'soldiers', they were making up the numbers and being killed in the name of Saddam. If they were lucky and didn't die in the first barrage of fighting, they would stand in the trenches too narrow to walk side by side, hungry and exhausted, defending their positions again and again. No retreat was tolerated and many men were shot having tried to run in the opposite direction. The enemy was just not giving up and Hakim was becoming used to the sight of the young Iranian soldiers reading the Quran out loud whilst walking through the minefields directly into their machine-gun fire clutching their dog tags like passports to paradise promised by Khomeini. They battled with constant hunger and thirst. The gas attacks were the worst. He could see the fear in his friends' eyes when they checked one another's gas masks. In those moments he rubbed the stone from the river the hardest and in the years that followed its surface became polished and smooth.

They held a position near the border and been under attack for more than three hours when a break in the fighting made Amir peer over the sandbags to have a better look. A goat appeared from nowhere and Amir, throwing caution to the wind, started to climb out of the trench before Hakim could reach for him. He was shot.

When Hakim returned from the trenches in 1988, the only thought that had kept him alive during that awful time was to be with her. He promised her before the war that he would come back and marry her. Nazreen promised she would wait for his return and if he wasn't coming back, she was never going to marry anybody else. Hakim sent a letter to her father asking for her hand in marriage when Amir was killed. He promised to look after the family like a son. Her father replied. He still carried the letter in his belongings. The letter was short. Never, it said. He was Sunni, she was Shia.

Hakim didn't understand why that made a difference. It never made a difference before. Was Hakim not a lifelong friend of her brother? Did Hakim not fight and share the little food there was with Shia? Because of a battle that took place hundreds of years ago? Because they couldn't decide who was the true ruler of all Muslims after the death of the Prophet

Mohammed? Were they not all Muslims? Did they not look out for each other in the trenches? Did they not face the enemy together?

Was it not Hakim who carried Amir to safety, when he was wounded in battle? Was he not the one who held his hand as he lay in agony, shouting for his mother, bleeding into the desert sand? Hakim promised his dying friend that he would look after the family. It was Hakim who carried his friend's body away from the enemy and paid for him to be sent home so he could be buried, instead of ending up in an unmarked grave on the battlefield which they had just lost again to the Iranians.

He didn't understand why her father couldn't accept him. Hakim would look after them, he would be the son that they had lost and provide for their daughter. He was the only man who would love and respect her as the woman he imagined she had become. Nobody was worthier of her than him. As he touched the stone in his pocket on the train home, he thought that the war had been for nothing. The borders were still the same and millions of lives had been lost but he wasn't going to let Amir's death be in vain. He turned up on her father's doorstep when the war was over and was met with fury.

'You,' he said and Hakim could hear the hatred in his voice. 'What do you want? I forbid you to come here. If you have come to see Nazreen, you're too late.' His eyes were blazing and he pulled back his head and let out a shrill cry of triumph. 'Nazreen married a year ago and was sent to a village near Basra with her husband. How dare you come to my house and presume you can take Amir's place?'

Hakim stood in the dirt and couldn't believe the betrayal. How could she marry somebody when they had made a pact all those years ago? He knew she wouldn't have married somebody else. It was her father's fault. He never liked Hakim and blamed him for the death of his son. Her father did the only thing he knew would hurt Hakim beyond all else. He began to feel the rage ascend in his body and his hands curled into fists.

'Get out of here and never show your face again,' her father screamed. 'I told Nazreen you died along with her brother. She was never going to be yours. Did you think you could fool me?' her father shouted, spittle running down the side of his mouth. 'Who do you think you are? Be gone or I shoot you like the dog you are,' he said and leaned closer towards Hakim's face.

'I will show you who I am,' Hakim replied and took a step towards Nazreen's father. He raised his fist to his opponent's face but thought better of it when his eyes fell on her mother in the yard behind. She was crying silently.

'I will see you again,' he hissed instead through gritted teeth. He picked up his belongings and left for his father's house. Hakim knocked on the door and a familiar-looking man opened the door to him.

'*Salaam Alaikum*,' the man said to him in greeting. '*Wa-Alaikum-Salaam*,' he replied, trying to see into the dark room behind the man.

'Is my father not at home?'

'Oh,' the man said, 'Hakim. I almost didn't recognise you. Please come in. I'm glad to see you well. Do you remember me?'

'Please sir, I want to know where my father is. What happened to him. Is he all right?'

The man took him by the hand and pulled him into the house. One of his children took the dusty bag of his shoulders and his wife made him sit down. She put a hot cup of mint tea in front of him and left. Hakim pushed the cup away and looked at the man with pleading eyes.

'Tell me where my father is.'

'I'm sorry Hakim but your father is dead. My name is Sadiq, do you remember? I lived in the house next door with my family.' Hakim nodded his head in recognition. 'Your father, Allah have mercy on his soul, was arrested last year and interrogated after somebody denounced him. When they released him two days later, we found him collapsed at the end of the street. He must have walked all the way back home. My wife looked after your father but his wounds were so severe that he died of his injuries a few days later. We had to promise him that we move into this house to look after it for you. I'm truly sorry. He was a good man.'

Hakim sat back in silence.

'Why didn't anybody let me know? I should've been here.' Tears welled up in his eyes and ran down his cheeks.

'Who denounced him, Sadiq?' he said quietly after a while. 'Who?' he asked louder.

'WHO, Sadiq,' he shouted at the man in front of him. He could see that the woman and their children were watching them now, frightened, huddled together at the back of the room by the back door ready to flee.

'I don't know, Hakim. I really don't. It was on the day after your friend Amir's funeral. I remember it because I spoke to your father after the internment. There had been a great many people. He looked pale and was very upset. He said he'd had a terrible fight with Amir's father but he didn't tell me why. The soldiers came for him in the middle of the night. I'm so sorry. I'll show you the place where we laid his body to rest if you wish, but for now you must rest.'

Sadiq stood up and held out his hand. He showed Hakim to his old room and shut the door quietly. Hakim lay on the mattress and stared at the ceiling. He silently started to cry for the loss of his father. It broke his heart to think that he couldn't say goodbye but his heart ached even more for Nazreen. How many times had he lain on the exact same spot dreaming of her? It was a lifetime ago and now everything was lost to him. Imagining himself in her embrace, clutching his blanket to his chest, he fell asleep.

Hakim woke the next morning feeling broken and exhausted. His heart was aching and he felt sick every time he thought of his father's mangled body. After breakfast, Sadiq accompanied him to the cemetery and pointed to an unmarked grave. He embraced Hakim. 'I will wait by the car so you can say your goodbye.'

Hakim sat down in the dirt and bowed his head at the foot of his father's resting place. He'd asked himself repeatedly who could have had a grudge against his father, who had always been kind and gentle. At first, he suspected Sadiq. His father's house was bigger after all but Sadiq's remark about the funeral the day before preyed heavily on his mind. He always came to the same conclusion. It pointed to one man full of hatred towards Hakim and his family. The longer he thought about it the more convinced he became that Amir's father was that person. He lifted his head to the sky. 'Father,' he said. 'I will avenge your death and take what is mine. I will find the culprit and make him suffer like you and I have suffered. I swear as Allah is my witness. One day,' he said to himself. 'One day.'

9.

Hakim travelled to Bagdad and found his father's cousin Abas. He joined the Republican Guard and worked his way up the ranks quickly. The only way to find out why his father had been interrogated and paid with his life was to find the paperwork. He was full of rage and vengeance and didn't care who he had to bribe, discredit or get rid of for that information. He became a willing tool, keeping Saddam in power and exterminating his enemies on the way. Saddam was paranoid about treachery and understood that if he showed weakness, his reign and life would be over. Everybody was a suspect. The Mukhabarat were everywhere and showed zero tolerance for any speech or prayer by the clerics that conflicted with the president's views. Neighbours reported neighbours who they begrudged and children unknowingly reported their parents to their teachers in class. Hakim witnessed torture and executions, sometimes playing his part.

He still hadn't found the name of the person who informed against his father but he had a good idea. There was only one way to find out and, on one of the mass arrests, Hakim made sure that Nazreen's father's name was on one of the lists. He was told by the arresting officer that the man he wanted for questioning had been put in a cell in the dungeons of Abu Ghraib prison, waiting for his orders.

He knew of the prison's reputation, he'd sent his fair share of men to be interrogated here. Built in the 1950s the building had been transformed from a maximum-security prison into a place of torture and death. When his van sped through the gates of the outer wall, he was surprised by the sight of the yard crowded with hundreds of men trying to stand straight in the desert sun. He saw one prisoner fall to his knees and heard a shot by one of the guards. The body was dragged off the square by two prisoners to a pile of bodies by the wall. Executions were a daily occurrence. They didn't bother to send the bodies home to the families now but instead piled them into mass graves outside the prison walls.

Hakim was shown to a windowless room and watched the interrogation of the man who he held responsible. When he arrived, the room was almost in darkness with only one light shining brightly on the figure of a man with his hands tied up behind his back. His head was lolling from side to side against his chest and he was bleeding from his mouth and nose. He sat on the only chair in the room. Hakim stood in the shadows, observing from a distance. How he wanted to take revenge himself, revenge on the man who he suspected was responsible for his father's death, denied him Nazreen and made him into the man he had become. An eye for an eye.

The interrogators had beaten her father's face and the soles of his feet till they bled. They hung him to a hook in the ceiling like a carcass, hands above his head, his toes barely touching the floor. They sent electric shocks to his body, supplied by a handheld battery. Cables were attached to his testicles. He had confessed to the denunciation of Hakim's father and given him the name of the man Nazreen married but still Hakim didn't care. He wanted this man to suffer like he suffered. When her father fainted from pain, they threw a bucket of water in his face just so they could torture him some more. The screams of her father for mercy didn't reach his ears. He didn't smell the stench of his bowels emptying into his pants. He didn't see the urine running down his leg, leaving a big wet patch on the front, dripping off his toes and pooling in a puddle on the floor. They had taken his fingernails and his dignity and he confessed. Sometimes Hakim frightened himself when he looked at his own reflection in the mirror. There was no compassion. His eyes showed no emotion and his heart was cold and void of empathy.

Afterwards, Hakim climbed down the stairs to the dungeons, ignoring the pleading of the men begging for mercy in the adjacent cells. His eyes tried to focus in the darkness, trying to get a glimpse of the once proud man through the spyhole in the steel door. He unlocked the bolt and was overwhelmed by the coppery smell of drying blood and stale urine. His fingers turned the switch by the door and the cell was illuminated by a dim bulb in the ceiling. The interrogators had stripped her father naked before putting him in the tiny compartment no bigger than a dog's kennel. He lay in front of him on the wet floor, shackled to a chain in the wall. He shivered with cold and pain and was curled into a foetal position. He was struggling to raise his head of the floor when the door opened, trying to shield his eyes from the glare of the light. Hakim stood in the doorway and revelled in her father's pain.

'Do you remember me?' he asked.

Through bloodshot eyes and with broken teeth her father looked up and tried to focus on Hakim's face. Hakim saw that he struggled to remember at first but then he could see the recognition in his eyes. Hakim smiled.

'I promised you that I would see you again,' he said. 'It's too late for you, old man.' He spat next to the body on the floor. 'Your death warrant has been signed and I promise you that I will be there, watching and cheering, when they put the noose around your neck.' He crouched down and leaned closer to the old man's ear.

'And then I will go and find Nazreen.' Her father broke down and tears were streaming down his face.

'Please.' He grabbed Hakim's arm, trying to speak with blood pouring from his mouth, bloody spittle wetting Hakim's face. Hakim pulled away and wiped the blood from his cheek. He had to strain his ears to hear her father's words.

'Please don't hurt her. She's pregnant with my grandchild. Have mercy, Hakim.'

Hakim looked down on the battered and broken shell of the man who once stood before him, laughing at his misery.

'Like you had mercy when you informed on my father? You knew what they would do to him and still it didn't stop you.'

'I didn't, Hakim, I swear it. We had words but I didn't denounce him, you made me confess.'

'You're a coward. I know the truth in my heart and so do you. I have your confession, old man. It's upstairs right next to your death warrant.'

'You must believe me, I didn't. That confession is wrong. Have mercy.' He lay his head back on the floor exhausted and began to cry silently.

'I will do as I please and you will die and never know what I'm going to do to Nazreen. Maybe I'll carve your grandchild out of her body after I'm finished with her,' he said in a cold voice. He turned around, switched the light off and bolted the door. He wasn't happy about the news of the child. He would have to give it some thought. However, he was satisfied that her father would never know that he could never hurt Nazreen.

It was an early dawn and the sun's rays were making their way through the yard up to the gallows. They were busy that morning. Condemned men, guilty or not, stood next to each other waiting to be taken onto their final walk. Some were crying and had to be held up by the man standing next to them. Some were praying. Some were standing in their blood-soaked clothes in stunned silence as they accepted the inevitable. Hakim made sure that her father was one of the last men to be hanged. Although he was naked and battered, his face covered in dry blood and his hair sticking out from his head in a mess, her father tried to stand upright in the line behind all the other men. Hakim watched from the balcony on the first floor, stirring his tea slowly. He didn't like it. Her father wasn't supposed to have any pride left in his body.

The prisoners were pushed off the platform one by one. Some necks snapped with a crunch. Other bodies twitched, dangling down from the ropes, swinging from side to side, their feet performing a macabre dance of death before they were still.

Hakim watched Nazreen's father climb the ladder, taking uncertain steps towards the spot where the hangman waited. He refused to wear a hood. His eyes travelled over the bodies that laid at the bottom of the gallows. He searched the building in front of him and found Hakim. He nodded his head once at Hakim and focused on a spot in the distance. They tightened the noose around his neck.

'I am innocent! *Allahu Akbar*,' he managed to shout into the silence before he was pushed to his death, the sun illuminating his face. Hakim thought he saw him smile. He took a sip from his cup. The tea tasted bitter on his lips and he put the cup down in front of him. He'd had his revenge. Why didn't he feel the relief he longed for so badly?

10.

He couldn't wait to go to Basra to find Nazreen but before he could set off, he received orders with the rest of the army to invade Kuwait. High on adrenalin and faced with no resistance, he joined his troops in looting the wealthy neighbourhoods, arrested the inhabitants and burnt down their houses. Being at the top of Saddam's security forces made him extremely powerful. He had plenty of resources, even in Kuwait. He knew where Nazreen lived and sent a unit to Basra where he had her husband arrested. They searched the house but didn't find her; maybe she was visiting a neighbour. He had to go back.

The soldiers put her husband in one of the holding rooms in the airport lounge and Hakim planned his next move. He had to be quick. The coalition forces were knocking on the door. It wouldn't be long till the airport was overrun. The soldiers had already started the interrogation when Hakim opened the door to the room. They'd punched the man's face when they arrested him and the dried blood had left a rusty streak from the bottom of his nose to the side of his ear where he tried to wipe himself. A pool of blood was drying on the front of his dishdasha.

Hakim frowned. This was the man her father had chosen over him? Impossible. The man in front of him was at least forty, chubby and looked pathetic. He smelled of sheep dung. His hair was receding at both sides and Hakim could see the skin shining through on the top of his skull where he was going bald. He didn't look like the man he imagined. He was a peasant. His clothes were shabby and dirty, he didn't even have proper shoes.

The man turned towards him when he entered the room and Hakim saw beads of sweat accumulating on his forehead. Big drops of it were running down the side of his face and into his eyes, blurring his vision and causing him to squint constantly. He extended his fat little fingers towards him, blinking and pleading.

'Please. Help me, sir. Why was I arrested? I don't understand. These men came and took me without any explanation. I've done nothing wrong. Look what they've done to me.' He pointed to his bloody nose. 'I'm...'

Hakim cut him short with a gesture of his hand. 'I'm taking him,' he said to the soldiers. 'This prisoner is to be moved to a different location. Orders from the top.' He yanked the prisoner off the chair, took him by the elbow and marched him down the corridor. Her husband continued to plead with him, shuffling beside him through the corridors down the stairs.

'Be quiet or I will shoot you right here.' Hakim reached behind and opened the clip to his gun. The man fell silent. Outside the building he started to plead with Hakim again.

'Please,' he said, 'I have a family. I have done nothing wrong. Why are you arresting me?' He pulled his sleeve up and showed Hakim a bangle on his arm.

'You can have this if you let me go. It's gold and very valuable.'

Hakim turned towards the little man, he swallowed the anger that was rising in his body. 'I am sure this will all be sorted in no time. There is no need to be afraid. We are taking you back to Basra.' The prisoner burst into a tirade of thanks. Eyeing his captor's uniform, he silently wondered if Allah was really going to be merciful.

Hakim had planned his escape from Kuwait ever since he arrived. In the last four weeks the coalition forces had been attacking from the air. It had been relentless and some of their bases were destroyed. He was in attendance when Saddam decided to release the foreigners and put them on a plane in a last attempt to avoid a conflict and to show the world that he wasn't the monster everybody thought he was, but it didn't make any difference.

Hakim had written himself a fictitious order so he could transport the prisoner to Basra for further interrogation. His driver was waiting for him and deposited his bag with looted jewellery and gold into the boot of the Toyota Landcruiser. They drove out of the parking lot of the airport, passed the gates and out through the town. Some districts were set alight in the hope that the smoke would distract the Allies from further attacks. He shut off the air conditioning when they had to pass between the houses, the fumes were choking him. When he looked to the east, he could see the clouds of smoke drifting in and out of town with the wind.

Hakim instructed his driver to head to Highway 80, the road to Basra and then to join Highway 8. There were less checkpoints.

They drove for a couple of hours and were close to the Iraqi border. The sun was high in the sky when Hakim told his driver to stop the car. He opened the back door and waved his hand at the prisoner to get out. It was too late for her husband to plead for mercy when he spotted the gun being pointed at his head. Hakim saw his mouth forming a silent 'but' before the bullet entered his head killing him instantly by the side of the road. He walked over to his driver and ordered him out of the car.

'I can't afford a witness,' he said and shot him.

Hakim looked up and down the road but there were no cars driving towards him from either direction. He took the driver's ID and the bracelet from her husband. Their bodies became nameless. He didn't even bother digging two graves or try to conceal them. The war was going to do the rest. How many men, women and children would never be identified? Casualties of war. There were going to be many. Convincing her to come with him was going to be more difficult. He put the car into gear and steered back onto the road, speeding up, leaving the bodies far behind. There was little time left.

At the border crossing nobody challenged him. His uniform gave him all the authority he needed, it made him powerful and feared. The soldiers at the checkpoints on the road to Basra waved him through with only a glance at his uniform. Nobody dared to look him in the eyes. He raced down the road with terror in his heart that her house might have been bombed. He knew he was ahead of the coalition troops but was he also ahead of a retreating Iraqi Army?

Looking back over his shoulder he saw big plumes of black smoke in the distance and knew that the oilfields were being set on fire and crude oil was being pumped into the sea. Those were the orders of Saddam. He could smell the burning petrol in the air and switched the air conditioning off. 'Please,' he prayed. 'Let her be safe.' He promised himself to become a better person. He was going to make up for all the murder he committed. Hakim was going to die a happy man if he could only see and hold her one more time. He needed to let her know how much he still loved her. He drove like the Devil himself was after him.

He reached the outskirts of Basra and turned his car onto the dirt track leading to the house. It looked intact. He was jubilant, his heart was racing. 'Please let her be at home.' He spotted her in front of the house. She had her back to him, holding a bundle of firewood. At that moment he could have cried with relief. With her hand on the door she suddenly stopped and lifted her head, turning it to the side, listening. She spun around, her eyes full of fear looking at the car speeding towards her.

She dropped the firewood to the ground and instinctively put her hands over her belly to shield it from harm. She didn't look at the man behind the wheel, her eyes were focused on the uniform he was wearing and she collapsed in front of his eyes into a heap on the ground. The car screeched to a halt. He ran towards her and scooped her up in his arms. He kicked the door open and took her inside where he laid her gently on the only mattress in the room. He stared at her belly. 'What now?' he asked himself and sat beside her. He needed to think.

11.

She didn't know how long she was unconscious but when she slowly opened her eyes she stared at the uniform, not the man wearing it. She recognized the uniform and started to panic, trying to lift herself up, looking for an escape. The last time she saw this type of uniform was on the day she had visited her parents' house in July last year.

When her father opened the door that day, the man wearing it had punched him squarely in the face and dragged his unconscious body to the waiting van. He opened the doors and they lifted his body off the floor and threw him in the back of the van, slamming the doors shut with a bang. Her mother pushed her to one side and followed the soldier, shaking her hands over her head in despair, pleading with the man that they had the wrong person. Her husband was innocent.

She pulled at the soldier's uniform, batting her tiny fists against his back. The man laughed, turned around and pushed her in the chest. 'That's what everybody says at first, you stupid woman.' Still laughing he pulled out his gun and shot her mother right in front of her eyes. From a slit through the shutters she saw her stumble backwards, trying to keep her balance, clutching her hands over the place where the bullet entered her body. With blood spilling through her fingers she collapsed, first forward onto her knees, then backwards till she lay on the ground, her knees bending at an unnatural angle, one hand stretching out towards the house. Nazreen saw her fingers move as if she was waving goodbye. Her mother's head rolled to one side and she closed her eyes. She was dead.

Nazreen put both hands in front of her mouth so as not to scream. She would have run out of the house and thrown herself over her mother's body, if it wasn't for the child she was carrying. She had no doubt that the soldiers would have shown no mercy towards her. She would have been just as dead as her mother, whose red blood was soaking into the dirt. The soldier who had shot her mother, kicked her body with his heavy boot. 'Peasant,' he said, spitting into the sand next to her. He looked around to see if there were any more challengers. Satisfied, he

62

shouted an order and the van sped off with her father's body inside. Nazreen had no doubt that she would never see him again.

After her initial shock and when she was certain that all the soldiers had truly gone, she left the house and sank to her knees next to her mother's body. She laid her head onto her mother's chest and wept quietly, still expecting the soldiers to return. There she remained until she realised that the sun was about to set. She hoisted her mother's body off the floor and dragged her into the house, where she placed her on the rug in the living room.

'*Inna lillahi wa inna ilayhi raji'un.*' ('Verily we belong to Allah, and truly to Him we shall return.') She spoke the words softly.

12.

Looking at her mother's body she pondered on how death made a person look so much smaller, their faces unreal, almost doll like and waxen. She covered her body with a blanket, got up and walked into the garden. She moved the old wooden bench from under the fig tree that her mother planted all those years ago. This had been her favourite spot.

They would sit together in the afternoon after school, before she had to do her chores. They would talk there, sheltered from the sun by the big leaves and she would tell Nazreen how she met her father.

'I never spoke to your father before we got married, you know. All I had was a picture of him, sitting on a chair with your grandparents on either side. He looked stiff in the picture but his eyes were kind. I trusted your grandfather.'

'Did you love my father when you met him?' she asked.

'Not then but I think I grew to love him when I gave birth to your brother. That was the best day of my life, *Habibi*, till, after all the miscarriages, I had you of course.' And she stroked over Nazreen's hair.

'You will marry one day and have children of your own.'

'I am going to marry Hakim, Mother. I love him.' Her mother looked at her with sadness in her eyes.

'You are far too young to know what love is, child, your father will decide what is best for you,' she said. The words echoed in Nazreen's head and tears started running down her face. She sighed and picked up the shovel, dug a hole under the tree as deep as the sun-baked earth allowed her to. The top, where her mother had raked came away quite easily but she had to fetch the pickaxe from the shed to loosen the earth further to dig a shallow space. She went back to the shed, fetched the wheelbarrow and collected all the stones her mother had placed around the irrigation ditches of her vegetable patches. She looked at the pile of stones at her feet. 'That will have to do,' she said to herself and returned to the living room.

She stripped her mother of the blood-soaked clothes and washed her body. As if in trance she repeated it three times. Upper right side, upper left side, lower right side, lower left side. She fetched a bowl of water and washed her mother's hair, wondering when her mother had gone so grey. Nazreen braided her hair into three braids, like she had seen her mother do when her grandmother passed away. She wiped the tears that were falling onto her mother's forehead with care.

Then she placed her mother's body on the sheets she had found in a trunk in her bedroom. She dressed her in an ankle-length sleeveless dress from the wardrobe and put on the matching head veil. She never saw her mother in that dress but she recognised it from the wedding photograph on the wall in the bedroom. It still fitted her. She placed her mother's left hand on her chest and covered it with the right hand as if in prayer. She stood up and looked down at her mother's figure. She didn't think she had ever seen her look more serene and beautiful in life.

She folded the sheets over her body, first the right side and then the left, until all the sheets covered her and secured the shroud with rope. Then she stood still, looking down at her mother's covered remains, pondering on what to do next. There were no male members of her family or friends present, so, facing Mecca, she performed the Salat al-Janazah, the funeral prayer.

'*Bismillla wa ala millati rasulilllah.*' ('In the name of Allah and in the faith of the Messenger of Allah.')

'*Allahu Akbar,*' she began. Looking at the Quran in front of her she tried to find the words.

'O God forgive our living and our dead, those who are present among us and those who are absent, our young and our old, our males and our females.'

'O God, whoever You keep alive, keep him alive in Islam, and whoever you cause to die, cause him to die in faith.'

'O God do not deprive us of the reward and do not cause us to go astray after this.'

'O God, forgive her and have mercy on her, keep her safe and sound and forgive her, honour her rest and ease her entrance; wash her with water and snow and hail, and cleanse her of sin as a white garment is cleansed of dirt.'

'O God give her a home better than her home and a family better than her family.'

'O God admit her to Paradise and protect her from torment of the grave and the torment of Hell-fire; make her grave spacious and fill it with light.'

Nazreen fetched the wheelbarrow from the shed and lifted her mother's lifeless body into it. She was larger than life when she was alive but weighed next to nothing in death. Tears welled up in Nazreen's eyes. She wiped them away with her sleeve.

She wheeled the body past the shed, passed the vegetable garden her mother had loved so much. She lifted the body from the wheelbarrow and stepped into the hole. She placed her mother gently onto the floor and turned the body, so it was laid on the right side, her face towards the Kaaba in the great Mosque of Mecca. Then, she uncovered the right side of her mother's face. She placed a sheet of wood over her body and covered it with earth. She laid the stones on top. Once the grave had been secured, she sat quietly by its side, hoping she had done it right and her mother could rest in peace. She got to her feet and sat on the bench, looking at the pile of stones in front of her.

'Until we see each other again in Paradise, on the Day of Judgement,' she whispered. She got up and placed the bench over the spot where her mother laid. Overcome with sadness and grief, exhausted from the burial, she laid on her mother's bed and cried herself to sleep.

The next day she packed her bags, stuffed it with her mother's belongings. It didn't amount to much. She took the wedding picture of the wall and a found a picture of all four of them in happier times in the trunk next to a box with her mother's jewellery. She returned to Basra on the train, always looking over her shoulder, making sure that nobody was following her, hoping she would get home safe.

13.

She lived in a small dwelling with her husband on the outskirts of Basra. Her marriage had been arranged three weeks after her brother's death. She hoped that she would see Hakim at the funeral but he didn't come. She knew he had sent a letter to her father from the front line. A cleric passed the letter to her father after the ceremony. Her father went mad after reading it.

'Who does he think he is?' he shouted, tearing the letter into little strips of paper, pacing back and forth in the courtyard like a caged tiger. He turned towards her with blazing eyes.

'What have you been up to behind my back?' he hissed.

Not waiting for an answer, he flew into a rage, grabbed her by the throat and pulled her off the rug. He slapped her twice across her cheeks and punched her in the face nearly knocking her unconscious. He dropped her on the floor. Her mother flung herself forward, trying to shield her from her father's anger. He took his sandal off and tried to hit her with it, bringing it down full force on her mother's back.

'Nothing!' she screamed, trying to get away from underneath her mother she pushed her to one side and rose to her feet.

'We have done nothing!' she screamed. 'I love him.'

Her father's face flushed red with anger and he looked around to where his hunting rifle was hanging near the door. He snatched it off the nail and pointed it at her with bloodshot eyes.

'You whore!' he screamed. 'You should be dead instead of your brother.'

With that he fired a shot but it missed and embedded itself into the wall behind her. Her mother screamed and lunged herself at him. He tried to shoot a second time but her mother grabbed hold of the barrel, pointing it upwards so the bullet fired into the ceiling. Bits of dust were landing on her hair. Her father pointed the gun at her for the third time and her mother grabbed the barrel with both hands, forcing it backwards at her husband with all the force she could muster and the butt hit him in the nose. Her father dropped the gun and covered his nose with his hands. Blood was streaming down his face. He crashed to the floor and her mother screamed at her to get out of the house.

'Go, Nazreen, go. He'll kill you. Quick, Nazreen, get out of the house. Go, go!' She pushed Nazreen backwards towards the door to the garden and Nazreen fled into the shed, barricading the door behind her with the wheelbarrow.

It took most of the night and she had fallen asleep on the dirty floor when her mother told her to come back in. She didn't know how her mother had persuaded her father to let her back into the house but her punishment was to be locked up in her room. A week later she was engaged to a man who was triple her age and whose wife had died recently in dubious circumstances. She didn't receive a picture of her suitor like her mother had done. She told Nazreen that she had brought shame to her father and the family and couldn't stay close by for fear of the town's gossip.

'Umi, I've done nothing to shame this family. I'm pure,' Nazreen pleaded with her mother. 'I don't deserve to be sent away from you. Hakim is going to marry me! Umi, help me, please. I can't marry the man Father chose for me. Please speak to Father, I'm begging you.' She flung herself to the floor and clung to her mother's feet. She refused the food her mother brought her in the hope to change her mind but to no avail.

Her 'fiancé' had come all the way from Basra to Baghdad and she was shocked at her father's cruelty. Their marriage was sealed. She returned to Basra with him, full of sadness for Hakim and herself. She wrote a letter to Hakim and asked her mother to pass it on if she ever saw him again. She wrote that she would always love him and she hoped that he would understand that she had no say in this marriage. She asked him to forget her and she released him from his promise.

Her husband made sure from the minute they entered the house what he expected of her. He wanted a woman who would cook and clean and give him children. She was not allowed visitors. She was not allowed to go into town, unless he accompanied her. She was not allowed nice clothes. The only thing of value she possessed was a bracelet he had given her on their wedding day. When he lay on top of her at night, sweating and rubbing his bulky body against hers moaning, Nazreen would switch her mind off till it was over. It hurt the first time he entered her body and it wasn't the wonderful experience she had been promised by her mother.

Was this the love her mother talked about? 'Make the marriage work and you will find love.' Those were the parting words her mother whispered in her ear when she kissed her goodbye at the train station. In time she could not recollect Hakim's face and he started to fade in her memory.

Her husband started to beat her with his sandal the first time she spilled his tea. He beat her with his fist the next time she didn't cook a meal to his wishes. He would beat her more every month she found out that she wasn't pregnant. He read the letters to her mother. So, she lied. She told her mother that she was happy and that her husband was everything she ever wished for. Why should her mother suffer like she did? Sometimes she wished her father had killed her that day. Three years passed and she was finally expecting, she cried for days. He changed after that and he beat her less and never as hard for fear of her losing the child. He even let her visit her parents to give them the good news.

Returning from the fields a week ago, a jeep had parked up front and soldiers were searching the sheds. They dragged her husband from the house, his wrists tied together with cable ties. She didn't know what to do. She didn't want to end up dead in the street like her mother, so she hid out of sight behind an olive tree and waited for the soldiers to leave. They left after searching the house and took her husband with them. She was so frightened that she spent half the night outside, hiding in the shed with only the sheep for company. When she was sure that the soldiers would not return, she made her way back into the house.

She sat on her rug, her back against the cushions, thinking. Should she go into town and inquire after her husband? Should she stay and see if he would return? What was going to happen to her and her child? Should she just pick some belongings and run? She felt helpless and was overcome with fear of the consequences of leaving him and where would she run to? she thought, as she drifted off to sleep. She woke the next morning and collected some firewood. Her husband still wasn't home but she knew he would beat her if there wasn't a fire in the oven and the tea wasn't made. She was just about to open the door when she heard a car approaching from behind. It was travelling at speed. She turned around, saw the uniform and then, nothing.

14.

Nazreen didn't know what to do. He had put her head on a cushion. She could see the man pacing up and down in front of her through her thick lashes and asked herself why she was still alive. She couldn't pretend to be unconscious any longer and slowly opened her eyes. She looked over to the man, standing in front of the window with his back to her. Maybe, if she was quiet, she could reach the knife by the side of the fire. She had to try something.

He heard her efforts to roll over and turned around. 'Nazreen,' he said and, so as not to frighten her, walked slowly over to her side. 'He knows my name,' she thought, oh God be merciful. The man in the uniform held a glass of water in his outstretched hand and stepped closer. She started to scramble away from him as he bent down and started to scream.

'Help, somebody help me. Please!' There was nobody near to hear her screams. 'It's OK, I'm not going to hurt you,' he said. Yet she shrank away from the cup as if it was laced with poison. She swiped the cup from his hand and he took both her arms, holding her still.

'Nazreen, do you not recognize me? It's me, Hakim.'

Dumbfounded she stopped struggling with him and tried to digest the words he'd spoken. She hadn't thought of him in such a long time and now he was standing right in front of her, talking so fast, she couldn't understand a word.

'Hakim?' she said, trying to recognize the boy in the face of the man before her. Hakim picked the glass up, refilled it and handed it to her. This time she took it and sat up.

'How…?' She took a sip of the water, trying to find an answer in his face. 'How did you find me?' she asked.

He seemed on edge and she wondered why he was in such a state. He repeatedly looked over his shoulder towards the door and out of the window as if he expected someone to drive up the path. He stepped towards her and sat next to her on the floor.

'Please don't be alarmed,' he started, taking her hands. 'I'm here to protect you.'

He thought about what to tell her all the way in the car, on Highway 8. He needed her to trust him and hoped she remembered what they used to mean to each other. He would stay as close to the truth as possible. Hakim looked straight into her eyes and hoped she would believe him.

'They arrested your husband a few days ago,' he said.

'I know,' she replied, looking down at her hands folded in her lap. 'I saw the soldiers when they picked him up and hid behind a tree. What happened to him?'

'I don't know for sure but they were holding him in a room in the airport lounge when I left him.'

'You spoke to him?' She felt a little embarrassed that Hakim had seen the man her father chose over him.

'I left a note for you, Hakim. I tried to explain.' Tears started to well up in her eyes.

'Nazreen, don't cry, please.' There was a stab in his heart. 'She did love that pitiful excuse for a man,' he thought. 'It doesn't matter now.' Her husband was dead. He handed her a cloth so she could wipe her eyes.

'I didn't get a letter from your mother but I remember the name of your husband very well. Your father shouted his name at me when I came to pick you up after the war. Your husband's name was on a list, so was yours. I needed to do something. I'm here to take you away before they have a chance to come back for you.'

'I couldn't free him for you but if he's innocent he will be home soon.' Nazreen shook her head. 'He IS innocent of any crime against the government, Hakim.' She didn't know why she said it. Hakim's friendly face cracked a little when she came to her husband's defence so quickly. She couldn't tell him that he wasn't innocent of any crime against her. Not yet. Maybe never.

'Time will tell, Nazreen,' he said standing up. He turned around and looked out of the window, trying to get his emotions back under control. 'The infidel are nearly here. They will win. I'm sure our troops are already fleeing Kuwait. You are not safe here. I am your only chance to get out of here unharmed.'

'I promised your husband to keep you safe, till this war is over. Here,' he said and handed her a bangle. 'He gave this to me so you could pay me.'

She recognised the bangle immediately. It was from Mohamed. She had given it to him on their wedding day when she was still under the illusion that she was going to be able to love a man without knowing him. How wrong she had been but she wasn't going to tell Hakim how miserable her life had become. She didn't want his pity.

There was an inscription of their names on the inside and the date of their marriage. She had the same bangle but she'd seen a jeweller when she visited her parents who made hers smaller, so she could fit it around her baby's wrist.

Mohamed had pulled a stick out of the fire and burnt her on her thigh when he noticed the bangle had disappeared from her wrist on her return. It didn't matter that it was going to be a present for the baby.

Subconsciously, she started to rub the place on her thigh where the burn had left a scar. Turning the bracelet in her fingers she wondered if he really handed the bracelet to Hakim? She kind of doubted it since Mohamad was not a generous man, but why should she doubt the words of the friend she had known for so long, much longer than she'd ever been married? Mohamad probably handed it over because he knew that he could take it back from her after his return. His return. She shuddered.

Hakim saw the shudder and put a blanket around her shoulders. He knelt beside her. 'There is not much time left to get to safety and you need to make up your mind whether to stay here or go with me.'

'What will happen to you and your baby when the Americans arrive?' he said. 'They might show you mercy but who knows? The Iraqi troops will come through here as well and you won't be able to hide then. It is too dangerous to stay but it is your choice.' His facial expression back under control, he looked at her with a warm smile. Her fears began to subside.

'You frightened me to death,' she said instead, pointing at the uniform. 'My father was taken by soldiers in that uniform and one of them shot my mother in the street.' Tears welled up in her eyes and he took her hand in his, stroking it gently. He was genuinely shocked at the news of her mother's death. He didn't know that she was visiting when her father was arrested and her mother's death was unintentional. If he had known he would have punished the soldier responsible.

'I am so sorry, I liked your mother very much. She was like the mother I lost too early. I'm sorry for your loss, *Habibi*. I must wear this uniform. Without it we won't survive. I took it from a dead man, hence the blood.' Only then she noticed the splatters of blood on the front of it for the first time.

'Without this uniform I would've already been arrested and shot for desertion. I am a desk clerk and to leave my post and help you escape, I had to be bold. I will be dead if they catch up with me.' He looked at her impatiently, waiting for her answer.

'But where would we go?' she said, still deciding what to do. He was pacing up and down the room. After a minute he crouched down next to her.

'I thought we could hide in the marshes till the soldiers have passed. Once we know we are safe, we can take a boat up north, back to our village and hide till all of this is sorted out.

'There are details that I haven't thought about yet. All that matters to me is to get you to safety and keep you from harm, just like I promised Mohamed.'

Finally, hearing her husband's name, he received the answer he was longing for, although for a totally different reason. She was frightened.

'You will not regret it.' He jumped up and turned around with a smile on his face. 'Let me see what we can take from the cupboards.'

She closed her eyes and folded her hands over her belly. Looking at the bangle, turning it in her hands, she thought of the one she had made for the baby. The baby, she smiled.

'How was Mohamed when you saw him last?' she asked quietly. He stopped in the middle of rifling through her cupboards and turned around. He looked at her and hoped his face wasn't giving him away.

'He was unharmed, if that's what you mean,' he said with a straight face. 'He was concerned for your well-being.'

That didn't sound like the man she married but she didn't know anything any longer. 'I'm sure it won't be long till you see him again. They will have to let him go. He's innocent after all.'

She didn't want to see her husband again, ever. This was the chance she had been waiting for. Maybe Hakim would get her out and she could convince him to take care of her and her baby. She hoped she'd never have to lay eyes on her tormentor again. She hoped he would die. Watching Hakim struggle and wanting to get as far away from the house as she could, she got to her feet.

'Wait, I'll show you where everything is. It'll be quicker that way.'

15.

They filled the Landcruiser with only essentials: rice, beans, flour and a few cans of peaches. They rolled up a small mattress and stuffed it with blankets. There was plenty of water in a jerrycan, strapped to the back of the Landcruiser. He told her to sit on the floor of the car and covered her with the rug from the living room.

'If we are being stopped at a checkpoint be quiet and keep as still as you can. I know you are frightened and this is going to be hard for you but we can't afford to draw anyone's attention.' He gave her a reassuring smile and turned the ignition.

The mighty Euphrates ran right through Basra all the way up to the borders with Syria and Turkey, from where it originated. It had been used for transport since the days of the Ottoman Empire and was surrounded by lush marshlands, the Al-Hammar marshes. Reeds were covering its banks. The Ma'dan, Marsh Arabs, peacefully existed here in the river basin, living in floating houses made entirely of reeds, harvested from the open water.

The rafts the houses stood on were made of compact mud rushes and were built without nails, wood or glass. Water buffaloes were submerged and grazing peacefully in the water. Hakim thought about whether they would be welcome in the *mudhif*, the tribal guest house, but then dismissed the idea. It would be a risk he wasn't willing to take. If they were lucky the reeds would give them shelter till the armies, whether it be Iraqi or Coalition, had passed.

Hakim concealed the Landcruiser behind a crumbling and abandoned shack on the banks of the river. He hoped they would be able to keep using the car until they were far away from Basra but they would soon run out of petrol. He helped Nazreen out from under the rug and they filled some plastic bottles with water from the jerrycan.

He saw Nazreen lift her dress and tuck the ends under her breast. She waded into the water. It was cold and at times as high as her hip. He saw an ugly scar on the side of her thigh. He frowned and, remembering the dungeons in Abu Ghraib, he would have to ask her later how she came by such an injury. He wasn't aware that she'd ever been taken for questioning.

It was hard work wading through the brackish water, sinking ankle deep into the slushy mud at the bottom of the marsh. There was a foul smell in the air when the black sludge surfaced from the bottom of the murky river and she imagined crabs and fish nibbling at her feet. She saw hundreds of Jesus bugs, skating away in front of her when she disturbed the surface.

Eventually they made it onto a small island. Back on dry land, sitting together facing each other over a small fire he had dared to light, they dried their clothes. She watched a kingfisher, its blue and orange plumage glistening in the setting sun, fishing for his supper. On the opposite side of the small island she spotted a white heron stalking the shallow waters for fish, accompanied by countless frogs croaking their evening chorus. Dragonflies, their wings as see-through as veils of satin, clung to the reeds and clouds of mosquitos were gathering just above the water. Swarms of Iraq babblers were performing a noisy dance above their heads. It looked peaceful enough but they could smell the oil burning and tiny black drops were starting to settle on the ground.

The water for the tea started to boil. He filled their cups and threw some rice and beans in the remainder. It was still light but soon he would have to extinguish the flames for fear of discovery.

'Where have you been?' she asked after a while looking at him with those charcoal eyes. 'I hope life treated you well.'

She told him that she knew he had written to her father.

'He went berserk, you know,' she told him. 'He was like a madman and would have shot me dead if Mother hadn't knocked him out with the gun.

'I was confined to my room. My father took the key. I begged my mother to speak to him and hoped she could talk him round. The next day she wasn't allowed to see or speak to me. Mealtimes were held in silence. A week later my father opened the door and said I was to marry Mohamed. I wanted to die that day.' She looked down at her hands. 'It would have been better if I had died that day.'

She looked up at him. 'I wrote you a letter and my mother said she would try and give it to you but she can't have done. Everything happened so fast.' She spoke the words into the fire.

'My mother silently dressed me in new clothes one morning,' she said, the flames of the fire reflecting in her eyes. 'I was released from my room and before I knew it my father marched me over to Mohamad. I was too shocked to comprehend what was going to happen till it was too late. The only thing I remember is my mother's tears at the train station. The whole day I felt like I was in a trance, maybe they drugged me, I don't know. I fell asleep on the train and when I woke up, I was in Basra.'

He saw that she was exhausted. She had placed her scarf over her head, the water nearby made the air cold and damp. He fetched a blanket and draped it around her shoulders.

'He turned out to be a horrible man.' Her fingers touched the place on her leg where the wound had healed.

'Was it him who scarred your leg?' he asked. She didn't answer but she didn't need to. Hakim wished he had known before he shot Mohamed. He wouldn't have gotten away so lightly. He felt rage welling up in him and he took a deep breath.

'Both our lives would have been different if I had been allowed to marry you.' He shrugged his shoulders. 'I travelled to Baghdad and kept myself busy so there was no time for anything else, let alone a family. Try to get some sleep, Nazreen. You are safe here. I'll watch over you.'

It seemed she'd only closed her eyes for a few minutes when the roaring thunder of fighter jets ripped her from her slumber. She opened her eyes in terror; screaming for Hakim she scrambled to her feet. Her head went from left to right looking for an escape off the island, reciting verses from the Quran, her mother had taught her when she was a child. Her breathing was shallow and fast. She turned and started to run.

He caught her in his arms before she could reach the water and enveloped her into his embrace, stroking her hair and speaking softly in her ear. She wriggled in his arms, trying to free herself but his strong arms held her in a vice. Her head flew up and she let out a blood-curdling scream which was drowned out by the helicopters flying over their heads. They heard big explosions from the direction of Highway 80, heard the gunfire from the Apache helicopters and saw fireballs lighting up the sky.

He was certain then that the Coalition forces had taken the airport and they were chasing the fleeing army out of Kuwait back to Basra.

'Shhhhh, they can't harm you,' he tried to assure her. 'Nazreen! Nazreen look at me!'

She didn't hear him and continued to scream. One arm slipped his grip and she managed to scratch his face in an attempt to break free from his clutches. Her fingernails left red streaks at the side of his face and he felt them burn. He slapped her across the face and regretted it immediately.

'I'm sorry, Nazreen, please forgive me. Nazreen! Please stop!' She fell silent and her body went limp. He held her tight.

'We are nowhere near the bombing and for tonight we are safe. Trust me.' She tried to get her breathing under control; leaning her head against his chest she started to cry. He held her closer and could feel her tears soaking into his shirt.

'We will have to leave this place when it gets light and travel further north. Try to go back to sleep, Habibi. I will watch over you.' Hakim put her head in his lap, stroking her hair. He touched the nail marks on his cheek. They burnt like fire but not as bright as the shame he felt when he remembered hitting her across the face. He looked at the mark on her cheek.

'You are safe with me,' he whispered, at least he hoped she would be. He was angry with himself, angry with her parents, her husband, angry with the Republican Guards who didn't put up a bigger fight. He had also just witnessed the Coalition's firepower and was not surprised.

16.

Neither of them slept properly that night. The jets kept on coming and the bombs kept on falling but the planes, just as he had promised, attacked the highway and not the marshes. She woke from a nightmare, imagined seeing people trapped in their vehicles, smelling the burning flesh of their bodies consumed by flames. As soon as they were able to see the riverbank they picked up their belongings and left the island behind. The bombardment had stopped and the birds were resuming their morning song, announcing the dawn of a new day. They loaded the car and set off just as the first light crept over the reeds and the surface of the water started to glisten in the sun.

In the night, Hakim decided to ditch his original plan of sailing up the river and opted for the desert instead. They would be safer in the desert but they were running out of petrol and soon they would have to walk.

They passed a wooden cart on the side of the road and he stopped to see if it was usable. A Landcruiser would certainly be more conspicuous than a wooden cart pushed by a man and woman fleeing from Basra. Everything was going to be about deception. Its right wheel was damaged but otherwise it seemed intact. He tied it to the back of their vehicle and left the road. A few more miles and then he would ditch the car. Travelling at slow speed they disappeared into the desert.

Eventually, he stopped because the engine cut out. He repaired the broken wheel of the cart with the spare wheel from the Landcruiser. They transferred their belongings and he changed out of the uniform into a dishdasha, an ankle-length tunic and everyday pants, which he had found in a trunk in her bedroom. It didn't smell very appealing but it was better than the uniform.

He thought about leaving the uniform behind but stuffed it into the bottom of his bag instead along with his gun. He might need both again.

They walked for miles through the desert sand. It was a slow process and she was unsteady on her feet. After she stumbled and nearly fell, he set up camp behind a burnt-out tank and let her rest. They couldn't light a fire because he was sure he had seen fires in the distance. They shared a can of peaches instead and he let her sleep.

Watching over her he thought of the child she was carrying. He didn't know what to make of it. Could he love somebody else's child as if it was his own? He thought of the man who fathered the baby. Would he resent it once it was born and he had to share the love of his mother? If only the child was his. It would have made him the proudest man alive.

She stirred in her sleep and suddenly opened her eyes, frantically feeling for his hand, moaning in pain.

'I think it is time.' Her breathing was laboured.

At first, he didn't understand what she meant. Did she mean to get up and continue their journey? She'd only just settled down. When he saw her looking down at her gown, he realised what she was trying to tell him. She tried to find his face in the darkness. The moon appeared briefly from behind the clouds and he saw her eyes wide open with fear.

'I've had contractions for a while but I thought they would subside when I settled down for a rest.' She started to groan again, breathing heavily through her open mouth. He didn't know what to do. He had only ever seen people go out of this world, never coming into it.

'Nazreen. Are you sure the baby is coming now? There are fires in the distance. You must be quiet or they will find us and kill us. Please, Nazreen, can you not hold on a little while longer?'

She pushed him away and groaned. She was petrified and she sucked in the air when the next contraction took her breath away. She reached out, gathered her dress and stuffed it in her mouth. Her scream sounded muffled. She grabbed his hand and squeezed. He looked around but they were alone. It was only them and the stars above. There didn't seem to be a gap between her contractions at all and he thought it was wrong. How could he help her? They were in the middle of the desert. Should he run over to the fires for help? Would they arrest him and leave Nazreen in the desert to die?

He was still thinking about his options, holding onto her hand, wiping her face with his shirt when everything happened at once. She ripped the gag out of her mouth and screamed, her body convulsing. He let go of her hand and jumped up. He ran around the tank to see if anyone had heard. Returning to her side he pulled her clothes aside and looked between her legs. The baby's head was crowning.

'I can see the baby's head, Nazreen,' he whispered. She lifted her head of the floor and looked at him through her legs.

'It's not time yet,' were the last words she uttered before she lost consciousness.

17.

The next contraction pushed the baby's head further out. He placed his fingers around the baby's head and pulled hard with the contraction that followed. There was a lot of blood and fluid. His hands were covered in sticky goo and the blood was soaking into the desert sand. The baby was coated in white slime and blood. It was very small. He saw the baby draw a shallow breath and then it lay still in his arms.

He panicked. Breathing heavily, he put his ear on the baby's chest and next to its mouth, but he couldn't hear anything. He searched for the knife and cut the umbilical cord in the hope that would make her breathe.

'No, no, no please don't!' He sat down with the baby in his arms. What was he supposed to do? He stuck his finger in the baby's tiny mouth and tried to dislodge the obstacle he thought was blocking the airflow. He turned it on its front and rubbed its back. He listened again for any sign of life. Nothing. He froze and sat back next to Nazreen. Tears welled up in his eyes.

She was unaware of her surroundings since he had delivered the baby, drifting in and of consciousness. It was getting lighter and the bleeding didn't stop. He was frantic with worry that she would bleed to death. He rolled up a dress he found in her bag and stuffed it between her legs in the hope of making it stop. Then he wrapped the tiny body into a blanket and laid it gently into her arms.

If he lost her now, all would have been in vain. He couldn't wait for her to wake up and say goodbye to her child. She was getting weaker and weaker and needed help. If they stayed here she would certainly die. If they went to the people in the distance they would also die. He had no choice. He took the baby gently out of her embrace. When he returned from the desert, he hoped that she would forgive him.

He lifted Nazreen off the floor and gently lowered her down into the cart. She was mumbling incoherently and felt hot to the touch. He walked quietly past the fires glowing in the distance. With every step he prayed for the first time since he came back from the war and he meant every word. He asked Allah that they wouldn't be discovered, that he would let her live, that she would never discover his lies, that Allah willing, he would give her another child. Hakim would make her happy.

'Please Allah, don't take her away from me.' He looked up to the fading stars in the sky.

'Not here. Not now.'

18.

The girl stank, she didn't just smell awful. Nothing alive should smell like that. It was the stink of a bin full of rotting potatoes combined with the stench of human excrement. Amal was certainly going to faint if she breathed in through her nose. She remembered the bomb that hit the electricity supply to her district and it couldn't be restored. When her mother opened the fridge, after the sirens had sounded the end of the longest air raid, the meat had gone off. She gagged at the thought and a shiver ran down her spine.

She stepped away from the boat and tried to breathe in the fresh, clean air of the Mediterranean. She looked at the people, crammed together like animals, a bucket of water at either end but no bucket to relieve themselves. Misery and desperation was edged on their tired faces. It reminded her of sheep, rounded up and shipped across the Mediterranean for profit. There were probably 200 people on the boat built for only a half of them. Mostly men, but she also saw women clutching their children to their breasts. She wondered if all of them survived or if there had been fatalities, the bodies discarded at sea, possibly going to be washed up on the shores in time.

Looking at the girl in front of her, she remembered, and closing her eyes recalled her own family's desperation to escape from Iraq.

Her parents had been teachers, until the end of the Iranian war. Her father joined the Ba'ath Party and kept his job but her mother had to stop working and stay at home. Her mother often told stories about the naughty children in her class and that she was sad when she couldn't teach any longer. Apart from that she never complained. Amal didn't understand why she wasn't allowed to go to school and she had to stay at home.

'Miriam is going to school every day and she's a girl,' Amal said, stating the obvious. Miriam was her best friend and lived in the wealthier part of town close to the government buildings. Their mothers used to teach at the same school. Miriam's mum kept her job. She was Sunni and a member of the Party. Her mother sighed.

'There is not enough money to send you to a private school like Miriam, my angel,' she replied. When Amal was old enough her mother started to teach her at home. It was their secret but Amal would rather go to school like her friend. Her favourite subjects were Maths and English.

'One day we are going to send you to England to become a doctor,' her mother said when they sat together reading a book that was called *Wuthering Heights*, a book her father managed to find on the black market. He paid a lot of money for it. She imagined herself as a ghost floating around in a white sheet across the moors, whatever they were, haunting poor Heathcliff.

That was before 9/11. Her father came home early that day and they watched in horror when they saw the first plane crash into the towers followed shortly by a second one, and she shrieked in terror when the two towers collapsed, one after the other. Their president denied any involvement in the attacks and denied he had weapons of mass destruction but America, supported by their British Allies, linked the attacks to Iraq and declared war.

'George W Bush is going to finish what his father started all those years ago,' her father said. Officials had been sent to look for the evidence of those WMDs but to no avail.

'Nobody believes a liar, Amal,' her father concluded. 'There's going to be another war.' And he was right as usual.

The first of the Allied bombings started on the ninth of March 2003. She remembered that night clearly since she was going to go to Miriam's twelfth birthday that afternoon. The birthday present was wrapped in luminous green paper and waited on top of the table ready to be delivered. Amal chose it herself. Her mother had taken her to the local bazaar and she purchased a tiny white music box from one of the stalls. When she opened the lid, a ballerina in a pink tutu was twirling around on the tip of her toes. Underneath her was a secret compartment. Amal was too excited to go to sleep straight away but when she did, she dreamed about the little cakes covered in honey and almonds she was going to eat.

She woke up by a noise and looked at the clock, two forty-five. Morning prayer was not going to be for another few hours. She thought that the muezzin had the wrong time when she heard the speaker of the minaret crackle loudly from the mosque close by and she pulled the pillow over her head. She had never heard an air-raid siren before then, but she knew exactly what the sound was when they started screaming. She jumped out of bed in her pyjamas. Instead of finding shelter in the arms of her mother coming towards her, she ran straight past, out of the house and climbed the ladder that led to the roof.

Within minutes she saw anti-aircraft rockets fired into the air and heard planes roaring overhead. Bright flashes of light were illuminating the city where the planes dropped the bombs. It could have been her imagination but she thought that the house was shaking. Standing on the flat roof, seeing the impact of the bombs, it looked like the city was on fire. Her father came up behind her and stood next to her for a minute, mesmerised. Then he took her hand and led her from the roof, pulling her back into the house where he almost threw her in her crying mother's arms. Excited, she tried to wriggle out of her embrace, all the while trying to describe to her mother what she had witnessed but her mother wasn't listening. Amal wished she would stop crying. Nothing happened to her.

She didn't go to Miriam's birthday party the next day, didn't put on her best dress or eat Miriam's fancy cakes. She wasn't too upset about it. Truth be told, she selected the little ballerina in the box because she liked it herself and now, she didn't have to part with it. However, she didn't go anywhere after that night for months. Her father wanted to see if they could make it to a shelter but her mother didn't want to leave their belongings behind. She remembered the bombing of an air-raid shelter in the middle-class district of Amiriya in the first Gulf War. The first laser-guided bomb smashed through the concrete wall and the second one exploded deep inside killing hundreds of innocent women and children. Her mother heard stories in the market after, that the smell of burnt flesh stayed in the neighbourhood for days.

Amal sided with her mother. She didn't want to be underground anyway where it would be boring, dark and full of smelly people. It was far more exciting on the roof. When she managed to escape her parents, she could see the black plumes of smoke rising from the buildings in the distance. Night and day, she heard the planes fly towards the city, smelled their fumes. They were targeting government buildings and Saddam's palaces. She fleetingly thought of Miriam and wondered if she was unharmed. She wondered if she had to give the ballerina to her friend and wished that her house would be flattened by a bomb. Amal immediately regretted her thoughts and sent a small prayer to Allah for forgiveness.

One day she found leaflets on the roof, distributed by American planes flying overhead, warning people to stay indoors. When the bombs fell close by, she felt the building shake, cracks appeared in the ceiling and the picture of Saddam fell off the wall.

Being on the roof lost its appeal. She stayed indoors, huddled between her mother and father.

'Better to die together,' her mother said. They sat listening to the old radio; the TV broadcasting had stopped, hoping that the batteries weren't going to run out.

The airport had been captured and rumours surfaced that their president was dead. They were unaware that he was captured on camera and broadcast on television several days later. Saddam had been seen emerging from his bunker in the north of Baghdad, greeting people and assuring them of their victory.

A victory, however, did not come.

19.

A week after Miriam's missed birthday party many government buildings were occupied by American forces, however much of the north of Baghdad was still not secured. The fighting continued and spilled out into the outskirts of the city.

The liberated people of Baghdad, finally able to release their pent-up anger and hatred towards the government, started to vandalize portraits and statues of the former dictator. They had taken no time in ransacking Saddam's palaces and museums, breaking and stealing irreplaceable objects of history. They looted embassies, government-run factories, supermarkets and hospitals, taking anything they thought of value. Amal, as well as her mother, were too frightened to leave the house for fear of being raped or murdered.

There was no electricity or running water and with the sun burning down on the city it started to smell. The trucks that collected the sewage and rubbish simply stopped coming. The streets were filthy with litter and faeces. People threw their waste outside their front doors and windows onto the pavement below. When it rained the water rushed unhindered down the street, leaving big puddles of filth and piles of human excrement behind. From the roof, laying on her belly, hanging over the side of the wall she saw emaciated dogs rifling through the rubbish, fighting with one another for scraps. She fired stones at the fat rats scurrying over the piles of faeces from a slingshot she made. It seemed these were the only creatures that weren't starving and she wondered what they were feeding on. She wanted to kill one so they could have it for supper. She was starving and anything was better than nothing, but it was pointless. Even if she managed to kill one the dogs were probably going to beat her to it. Groups of men were roaming the neighbourhood looting houses and it was far too dangerous to leave the house. She could hear the men screaming at people stupid enough to open the door. They fired their guns in the air, shouting *'Allāhu Akbar'*, before they pulled the people from their houses into the street and ransacked their belongings.

Her father returned that evening carrying a half-empty cannister of water. He collected it from a tanker, guarded by British soldiers and he had queued up for it all day.

'How are we supposed to wash ourselves with that?' her mother said sitting at the table and looking at the pitiful amount of water in front of her.

'This is not for washing, Safiya, washing is a luxury we can't afford.'

'But I need to wash. These clothes are filthy and I smell like a goat. Think of Amal and all the diseases we could catch. We need to wash!' She stood up.

'That's it. I'm going to the river,' she exclaimed loudly.

Amal clapped her hands, excited with the prospect to escape her confinement. Maybe they could visit Miriam. The telephone lines were dead and they had not talked to each other since the day before her failed birthday party. She wasn't going to mention her present for sure. Her birthday had been and gone.

'You will do no such thing. I forbid it, do you hear me?' Her father's voice was getting louder. 'No woman's safe out there. Men have turned into animals. I forbid it, Safiya.' He slammed his fist on the table. 'You go out there and I will beat you.'

Her mother looked at him in shock. He'd never been violent towards her, never raised his voice. She nodded her head in agreement, tears in her eyes and sank onto the chair behind her. Quickly he sat down next to her, taking her hands.

'I'm sorry, Habibi. I just don't want you to get hurt. It's too dangerous out there. Today I saw a man being shot for a bag of groceries and nobody came to his aid, not even the police.'

He told Amal that whilst he was standing in line today, he overheard that a mob had broken into her beloved zoo. Men took the animals to be slaughtered for food. A lot of them died for lack of food and water. There was nobody taking care of them any more. She was heartbroken and cried herself to sleep that night, sending a prayer to Allah to punish the murderers.

The next day her father didn't return until the middle of the night. Her mother was out of her mind with worry and when he finally knocked on the door, she flung herself into his arms. He had to walk for hours till he stumbled across a crowd waiting for flour, handed out from a truck with a big blue UNICEF sign on the side, guarded by soldiers. The crowd was impatient and hungry and when they surged forward, the soldiers fired their guns.

'I saw the fear in the soldier's eyes, Amal. First, he shot in the air as a warning but the crowd kept coming towards them. Then he shot into the crowd. Two people were injured and taken to hospital.' Order was restored.

'Look,' he opened his satchel that normally contained his books. 'I have some flour.' Her mother shouted out with glee.

'I also have this,' and her father pulled a camping cooker out of the bag with a smile. 'I liberated it from an abandoned shop.' He handed it to his wife and her mother clutched the cooker to her chest, performing a little dance in the kitchen, which made Amal laugh. She hadn't seen her mother that happy in a while.

Amal was surprised at how inventive her mother could be. She mixed the flour with water and made a dough, put a pan lid upside down on top of the stove and lit it with a match.

Soon the smell of baked flatbreads was wafting through the house. It made her mouth water. Sitting by candlelight and sharing the bread with her family Amal felt almost normal.

'Did you know that they tore the statue of Saddam Hussein in Firdos Square from its plinth?' He looked at them, savouring every bite of his share of the bread that he had smothered in honey.

'The people were chipping away at the bottom of the plinth with hammers and shovels. It was getting them nowhere so the Americans who watched tore it down with the help of a tank.

'The crowd went hysterical, following the statue as it was being dragged through the street. They hit Saddam's head with their bare hands and the bottom of their sandals. Can you believe that?

'I was expecting the secret police to turn up and kill them all but nothing happened. It is the dawn of a new area. I'm telling you.' He licked his fingers and continued.

'I didn't like that the American flag was being draped around its neck though. Somebody should remind the Americans that they have liberated Iraq, not conquered it,' and he sat back folding his hands over his tummy. Amal slept well that night, dreaming of a new Iraq where she could go to school and where she wasn't hungry.

When it rained heavily on one of the following afternoons her mother took her up on the roof. Again, Amal thought her mother was ingenious. She hung sheets on the washing line and they both washed in the rain behind the makeshift curtain. Afterwards, her mother poured some water from the cannister and made tea. It tasted bitter because they'd run out of honey but the taste of the canned pineapple made up for it. Amal was in the middle of telling her mother about the rats when she saw her put a finger on her lips and motioned her to be quiet. They listened closely, heard car doors being opened and closed. Amal ran to the door and put her ear against the wood. She turned to her mother and motioned her to be quiet. With a finger she pointed to the roof and, before her mother could say anything in protest, she was gone.

The Americans, still searching for Saddam, were busy going from house to house in their district. Amal watched a column of vehicles approaching down the road from her vantage point. The soldiers jumped out of the Humvees, machine guns in hand, ready to fire. They didn't bother knocking to be let in but kicked the doors down with their heavy boots. Swarming into the house like angry wasps they searched every room from top to bottom. She was halfway down the ladder when she felt something being pushed into her back. She stopped, too frightened to climb down any further. She looked over her shoulder and saw the nuzzle of a gun pointing at her back. She put her hands in the air, trying hard to keep her balance.

'Please don't shoot,' she said.

The soldier, surprised to hear her speak in English, let her climb down completely and marched her back into the house. He searched her for weapons and confiscated her slingshot.

'Sit,' he commanded and pointed the gun at her mother sitting on the floor in the corner of the room fearing for her life.

'Does anyone else live here? Where is your father? Any brothers?'

'There is only my mother and my father has gone out to find food,' she replied. The soldier let go of Amal and she ran to her mother, taking her in her arms.

Satisfied with the search the soldier spoke into his headset and turned on his heels, ordering his men to leave the premises. Her mother burst into tears the moment the soldiers stepped back onto the street.

'I hope your father is going to be all right. I have never been more frightened in my life,' she said as she picked the clothes off the floor and put the mattress back on the beds. They didn't see her father until the next day. He had to hide from a gang of Shia militia and was too frightened to be seen. It was too dangerous to be out after dark.

The Americans continued their search. It was rumoured that Saddam was hiding near his home town of Tikrit, where he hoped he could still rely on the support of his tribe. They searched everywhere, sometimes twice in the same location and eventually discovered his hiding place in early December. Broadcasting had resumed at some point and electricity was supplied by generators installed by the army engineers for a few hours each day. She watched the news, sitting next to her father on the settee, as Saddam was pulled from his hidey hole in the ground. He looked like an old man and a shadow of his former self. Gaunt, with a big beard, his hair untidily sticking up in all directions he was arrested and put in American custody. He was charged and put on trial for crimes against humanity.

'Good riddance. You'll see, Amal,' her father said hugging her with one arm draped around her skinny shoulders. 'Now that this evil tyrant has been disposed of life is going to change for the better. We will unite as one nation and put our differences behind us.

'To peace and prosperity.' He lifted his teacup and raised it in a toast towards the television. Amal had never seen him so happy. He let go of her and grabbed her mother round the waist, swirling her around in the room, grinning from ear to ear. Not wanting to be left out Amal joined her parents in their dance. Surely, she would be allowed to visit Miriam now the nightmare was over. It had been months and it would be nice to talk to somebody else than her parents. However, she never saw Miriam again. Her father found out that Miriam's family had fled the country to Jordan the day before the bombing started. It was so unfair. Miriam always got everything Amal ever wanted. A big house with a pool, a private school and now freedom. Just before she fell asleep her eyes moved over the little box with the ballerina inside. Her fingers stroked the surface of the lid and she smiled.

They danced too soon. Saddam had controlled his people through fear and terror but the new government failed to find a solution to unite all the parties and tribes involved in building a new country. Nothing was being achieved. Corruption was still as common as it had been before. Shia retaliated against Sunni and vice versa. Men who had formerly been friends, united in hatred against the government, were now enemies. The Coalition forces could not think of any other solution than to separate them from one another. They imposed a night-time curfew in the hope of keeping Shia and Sunni from killing each other.

But the division was too great. Suicide attacks in the markets became a daily occurrence. The streets were running red with the blood of the innocent.

20.

Inga folded the uniform into a neat parcel, wrapped it in clingfilm and stuffed it into a plastic box that she had taken from the cupboard.

'I think those stains could be blood,' she said to her husband. 'I'm keeping it for evidence.'

'Inga, love, give it a rest. It's probably just rust from the zip. You and your bloody imagination.' Jonathan shook his head and rolled his eyes.

'Why should I give it a rest? That evil man ruined my life and I need to know who buried the uniform in my allotment.' She jumped off her chair. 'Nothing is ever going to grow in that spot now. I'm sure of it.' Jonathan tried another approach.

'It was probably brought back as a trophy after the Gulf War. Do you remember that picture of Saddam you saw on *Posh Pawn* you told me about the other day?

'Whoever came back with it probably thought of making some money from the sale. When he saw there was no interest, he didn't know what to do with it. This can hardly be donated to charity. Can you imagine Mavis's face in the Help the Aged shop down the road when you tell her where it came from? Maybe his *wife* did not want to have it in the house but he couldn't part with it so he buried it on the allotment,' he continued.

She thought about it for a second. 'I hope you are not having a dig at your wife for not displaying all your trophies all over this house,' she snapped at him, looking over her glasses. 'Anyway, I think that's very unlikely. Why was it buried under the shed?' she emphasised 'under' with a scooping motion of her hands. 'Why not just put it in the bin? It doesn't make any sense, don't you see? Somebody hid it there because it's evil.'

He looked at her serious face and burst out laughing. 'That was funny. How can a piece of material be evil? You make me laugh.' She was convinced the uniform was evil and didn't find it funny at all. Why could he never take her seriously? She hated it when he didn't take her seriously.

'You think I'm stupid, don't you?' she asked. 'That's not what I meant. Of course I don't think a piece of cloth is evil but the person wearing it might have been. That's all. Don't you feel it?'

'Whatever, maybe the person who buried it wasn't the one who built the shed! Have you ever thought of that?' She pondered over his question for a minute.

'I hope you're not going to do anything stupid,' he mumbled under his breath, thinking she didn't hear him. She might be wearing glasses but she had the hearing of a cat.

'Like what?' she said.

'Like ringing the police.' He looked at her. 'Remember how it made you feel? You thought it made you a laughing stock of this neighbourhood and you thought everybody pointed their fingers at you behind your back. You were totally paranoid. It put you in a right mood and I had to listen to you for days.' Her face turned red at his remark.

'Thanks for reminding me.' She felt the embarrassment return from deep inside.

'OK, no police. I'll see if I can translate the paper myself. Since you seem to think it's Arabic, I will consult the Internet. If that won't do, I will go to the library and if I haven't got any luck there, I will get in contact with the local mosque. I promise not to ring the police again.'

He thought that was the end of the conversation until she turned towards him five minutes later with a smile.

'Do you know that they do drug testing kits on line? Maybe they have a blood testing kit on line too that I can use on those stains?'

He sighed heavily and shook his head. 'God help me,' he said.

The next morning, she retrieved the paper from the box. It had been difficult to unfold. The moisture in the ground and subsequent exposure to the warm air in her kitchen had stuck the folded page together. She thought of when she was a child and collected stamps. To get the stamp off the letter undamaged she used to hold it over steam. She wondered if moisture would do the same to the paper in her hand. She had to try.

She left it uncovered next to the dryer in the extension and switched it on. She wondered why so much steam was released from the dryer lately since the hose was connected to the outside but that was an investigation for another day. The escaping steam had done the trick. Carefully she pulled the corners apart. There the folds had ripped a little and she could see through the brittle page.

'I hope I haven't destroyed it completely,' she thought when she picked it up and had a closer look.

The writing was faded and she had difficulty to decipher the page. She wished she had a looking glass. At the top right-hand corner was a date. She pulled out her mobile phone and took a picture. She zoomed in on it. Even though it was blurry she could make out the date. It was published in April 1991. 'Something to get excited about,' she thought and clapped her hands. There was something you don't see every day. She held a snippet of a day in history in her hands. Looking at the date she immediately thought of her husband who returned from Iraq at the end of that month.

'How extraordinary,' she said to the dog laying at her feet and fetched her laptop.

21.

The initial excitement gave way to frustration. Inga tried but failed terribly to translate a single sentence. She had been hunched over her laptop for an hour and was overwhelmed by how complicated every single letter looked. Not being very patient she finally shut the lid of the laptop and sat back, staring into space. After a while she carefully slipped the paper into a plastic wallet and grabbed her car keys of the table. The dog jumped off the settee, wagging his tail in anticipation, he looked at her and nudged his lead.

'Not now, matey,' she said. 'Later.'

The dog looked at her in disgust. He walked past her, head hanging down and climbed the stairs to the bedroom where she knew he would be waiting for her return, sulking. She would have felt sorry for him on any other day but not today. Today she would solve the riddle of the newspaper article. 'The library it is,' she said looking at the paper in the wallet and left the house.

The librarian found a book called *Arabic writing for Beginners* but it left her deflated. There was so much to take in. A little squiggle over or below a letter seemed to give words different meanings. People often said to her that the German language was complicated and that she was lucky to be a natural speaker.

'These people should try Arabic,' she said to the library assistant who didn't have a clue who the people were she was referring to when she handed the book back. Inga didn't even know what she was looking for, it all looked the same. It could have been a book of spells for all she knew. All she had was a date. Aggravated, she stomped out of the library and rang Libby.

'Stop being so impatient!' Libby said when she answered the phone and listened to Inga's predicament.

'Rome wasn't built in a day, hun. If all fails you can always go to an official translating service. That's what I would do. Don't give up now. This is only the beginning of your adventure.'

It made her smile. Libby always thought of life as one big journey, full of adventures and secrets that needed to be uncovered. Problems were just temporary stumbling blocks.

'Shall we meet for lunch on Thursday? Then you can tell me all about it. You can do this. I believe in you.' Feeling better about herself Inga carried on.

Libby was right. She couldn't give up that easily. She had thought about going to an official translating service but that would cost money she was unwilling to spend at this stage. There had to be another way.

She crossed the road and entered the coffee shop opposite the library. She was always able to think better with a cuppa and a nice piece of cake. She looked at her watch. Was that the time already? She had spent half a day getting nowhere fast. Sitting in her favourite chair at the window watching the world go by, she suddenly slapped her forehead.

'I'm stupid, why didn't I think of that before?'

The answer to her quest had been right before her eyes. She drank her coffee in a hurry, which burnt her lips, wolfed the cake down, which would probably give her heartburn later and dashed out of the café. A traffic warden quickly put a ticket under her windscreen wiper when he saw her approaching.

'You're three minutes late, madam,' he said, looking at her sternly. She looked at him in disgust.

'Really? Three minutes? Can you not rip the ticket up this one time? It was only three minutes after all.' She battered her eyelashes. It always worked for Libby.

The warden looked at her shaking his head. 'Sorry, madam, I already issued the ticket and put it into my machine. It only costs £40 if you pay it in the next two weeks.' As if that knowledge would cheer her up. She was fuming. Three bloody minutes!

'Dickhead,' she thought and snatched the ticket from the windscreen.

'I will contest this in court, you know,' were her parting words, knowing full well that she was going to pay the fine straight after she got home. A few minutes later she parked the car in front of her daughter's house. She put the key in the door and let herself in.

'Hi, guys!' she shouted from the door. 'It's only me!'

Her daughter April emerged from the kitchen covered in flour. 'Mum.' She hugged her and kissed her on the cheek. 'What a nice surprise.' Her grandchildren came running out of the kitchen. They were licking the dough off a whisk.

'Nana!' they both screamed when they saw her and Inga bent down to receive their hugs and kisses. They dropped the whisks on the floor.

'Have you got a surprise?' they said and stripped her of her bag, rifling through its contents.

Inga looked up. 'Hi, darling. Are you baking?' Her daughter looked at her and laughed. 'Guilty as charged. What gave me away?'

Inga ignored her daughter's sarcasm. Why did nobody take her seriously? 'Any chance of a cuppa? I need a word with Atif. Is he here?'

Inga referred to April's lazy, waste of a space husband. He was born in Britain but his parents immigrated from Pakistan in the sixties. Inga called him her son-in-law even though he was not an 'in-law' in any legal sense of the expression. However, he was a Muslim, he read the Quran, the Quran was written in Arabic. Problem solved.

She never understood why April married that man. There was nothing wrong being a single mother these days. Did they not support her fully through the first pregnancy? After the initial shock they set her daughter up in a council house. Inga was there at the birth and cut the cord. It was magical. Atif was nowhere to be seen.

She felt cheated when, after a year, she found out their daughter married Atif in a religious ceremony and converted to Islam. April never mentioned her intentions once. Inga didn't know about it and hadn't been invited. It looked like her daughter had waited until Inga and her husband had left for their holidays. When she had touched on the subject on her return April asked if she would have come. Inga skirted around the subject in saying that she wasn't given a choice. They had agreed to disagree. She was even more shocked when she found out that her daughter was pregnant for the second time shortly after. Her husband gave up entirely on their daughter's state of mind until he held the little bundle for the first time and fell in love instantly.

Atif was a nice enough guy but he didn't understand the fundamental principle of being a good husband and father. Inga didn't understand why her daughter hadn't kicked him out permanently yet. Every time April had enough of him and made him leave, he wormed his way back into her life somehow. He was like a child that never grew up but, unlike Peter Pan, he was the real deal.

'I could really do with his help.'

Inga fabricated a story about the piece of paper in the wallet she was holding to her daughter's face.

'I found it in the garage amongst your father's army stuff. I asked him about it and he can't remember why he had it, or what it says. He claims that he probably used it for wiping his bum at the time.' Her daughter pulled back in disgust.

'Mother!' She swatted the bag away from her face. 'Get that thing away from me.'

Inga ignored her. 'It's covered in plastic silly. Do you think Atif could have a look and translate it for me?' April snorted.

'He can just about read the Quran in Arabic, Mum. He speaks Urdu but I doubt he can read an Arabic newspaper. It's a completely different language.'

'Crap.' Inga put a hand in front of her mouth and looked at her daughter, lifting her shoulders in regret. She turned around to her grandchildren. 'Whoops. Sorry guys, Nana said a naughty word.' Her oldest granddaughter looked over her shoulder without taking her eyes of the TV, shrugging her shoulders.

'No problem, Nana, Mummy says crap all the time.'

'Isn't that nice.' Inga gave her daughter the 'eyebrow'. She was able to lift one eyebrow higher than the other when she disapproved of something.

'Come on, Mum, it's nothing they don't hear on this street!' her daughter replied. 'I can show it to him when he comes back from wherever he is but don't hold your breath. Maybe he can show it to somebody at the mosque?'

'Not a bad idea, love. I'll leave it with you then.' Inga wasn't convinced but it was worth a try. She got up and sat between her grandchildren.

'I hope this cake is going to be ready soon. It smells awfully nice, doesn't it, girls?'

22.

On her way back to the house Inga decided to make a detour past the allotment. She hoped to speak to her neighbour. He might be able to tell her who leased the plot before she had taken the lease on. Pete was busy turning the soil in one of the raised beds when she popped her head over his gate.

'Pete!' she shouted. 'Have you got a minute?'

'Hi.' He smiled and waved for her to come in. 'Come in, come in. Don't be frightened of the dog. His bark is worse than his bite, you will see what I mean in a minute.' With that, he let go of the little Staff's collar. The dog ran towards her barking, frantically wagging his tail ten to the dozen.

'Hush little fellow,' she said, leaning down to pat him on the head. 'Aren't you an excitable, handsome little man?' The dog jumped up, trying to reach her face for a lick, knocking her over in the process. She landed on her bottom with a bump and the dog was all over her in an instant. Pete laughed, called him back to heel and handed him a treat from his pocket.

'He will calm down in a minute.' He stretched out his hand to help her get up. 'To what do I owe this pleasure? Are you going to tell me what was in the bag?'

'Sort of.' She smiled awkwardly and brushed the dirt from her bottom. 'I'm after some information really. It's in connection with the bag we found. I wondered if you can tell me whether you had any contact with the previous owner of my plot?'

'I certainly did,' he said and stuck the spade into the soil, cleaning his hands on a towel next to him. 'You better sit down. Have you got time for a coffee?'

Later that evening Inga told her husband about her day. She talked about how the Internet had let her down and how the trip to the library had been a waste of time. She told Jonathan at length how she argued with the warden for giving her a ticket for a parking violation of just three minutes.

'Three minutes! Can you believe that? He was probably waiting around the corner for it to run out, he was there that fast. Three bloody minutes, unbelievable.'

'Are you going to contest it then?'

'Well, no, I've paid it already.' Jonathan shook his head. 'I never expected anything different from you.'

'I know. I'm sorry. All mouth no trousers, that's me, I'm afraid. But that's why you love me.'

'I do but I'd rather not fork out forty pounds.' She quickly changed the subject. 'Anyway, I sat in the café and had an epiphany.' She told him about her theory.

'I told April you might have used it as toilet paper!' she shouted into the living room from the kitchen and giggled at her deception. 'Hopefully Atif will have more success than I.'

'Depends, if you want it translating any time this side of the year. You should have consulted a professional.'

'I might still have to, love, but for now I have hope in my heart.' She walked into the living room wiping her hands on a tea towel. 'Do you want to hear what Pete—'

'Who's Pete?' he interrupted her in midsentence.

'The guy who's got the plot next to ours. I've told you about him. He waited with me when they dug up the bag.' He grunted.

'You clearly never listen to me,' she complained. 'Anyway, as I was saying, do you want to know what he said about the previous owner?

'Pete had signed the lease to his plot in 2015. He recalled that the shed had already been there. A friendship developed with his neighbour. They shared the same hobbies and went fishing on the local reservoir every Saturday till it turned too cold for his friend. He was quite elderly but young at heart. His name was Wilfred and he had leased the plot ten years before him.

'Pete remembered how the plot had looked when he stepped through the gate for the first time.

'"It was beautiful' he said. "There was an arch over the path covered in yellow roses. The steps leading to the shed were bordered by beds of colourful flowers. They bloomed all summer long and the smell of rosemary and thyme from the herb garden at the bottom was overwhelming when we sat together for a game of chess after a long day. Every little terrace coming down the path was planted with different varieties of vegetables. He let me use his potting shed in the spring before I had my own and we even talked about building a smoke shed for the fish we caught. One night when we sat in front his shed on our camping chairs with a can of lager Wilf mentioned that the shed looked 'outlandish' when he first saw it.

"'From afar it looked like any other shed,' Wilfred had said. "On the inside though it was a different matter. I didn't know what to make of it when I saw it for the first time. Opposite the entrance door was a rectangular window frame made from plywood, I guess. It was painted in white and it turned into a kind of onion shape at the top. The onion was painted green and it had a gold crescent moon at the highest point of the dome. Come to think of it, it looked like the mosque you can see when you drive over the bypass." He took a swig of his lager. Wilfred was only allowed to drink on his allotment. There were different rules for him at home.

"'The wife booked a holiday to Turkey in the eighties once because it was cheap. We found out why the hotel was so cheap on the very first morning. You don't want to be near one of those minarets when they go off at all hours of the day. Worst holiday I ever had. We never went back after that experience. We chose to go to Majorca instead. Much quieter.

"'The window itself was covered by white shutters in a filigree pattern. I can only compare it to one of those radiator cover patterns that became popular in the nineties. When you opened the shutters, a painting was revealed. It was like an imaginary desert landscape of some sort. It had different-sized sand dunes in all kinds of light browns and yellows. There were palm trees at the bottom and the sun above the dunes was such a bright white I imagined it burning my face. I fought in the battle of El Alamein you know, so I should know.

"'The ceiling of the shed was painted dark and appeared to be almost black. It was covered in stars that would glow in the dark. The most astonishing things were the little stars in the picture next to the sun though. In the daytime the stars were hardly recognizable but at night they would gradually come to light and it seemed that the blazing sun turned into a full moon.

"'It somehow reminded me of the night before we went into battle for the second time, hoping to expel the Nazis from Egypt for good. We thought about the battle ahead and what the people at home expected of us. Sitting on the still warm sand most of us were in deep thought, looking at pictures of the people that we'd left behind. Would we ever see them and England again or would our bodies be buried in the desert sand? As the sun went down and the light started to fade, little by little, the stars appeared in the sky above. Looking up I wondered if my Daisy was looking at the same stars that night. Thinking of her left me with a strange feeling of calm in the middle of the mayhem around me.

"'But I'm telling you, Pete," he said "As God is my witness, that picture started to give me the heebie-jeebies. The picture could have been from *Arabian Nights*. When I looked at the stars appearing in front of me and the sun turn into a moon that night, I expected Scheherazade to pop up next to me, ready to tell me her story. It looked as if it was alive. My wife was amazed when I showed it to her. She wanted to keep it but I had too many bad memories of the War.

"'We had a right ding-dong over it, but I won in the end. I reminded her that the allotment was supposed to be for my pleasure. My sanctuary and a man's place. No women allowed. She didn't speak to me for a couple of days after but in my eyes that was no real punishment." Laughing, he choked on his next sip and Pete had to slap him on the back. Wilfred chuckled to himself when he had his breathing back under control.

"'Without her constant nagging, I enjoyed the peace and quiet at home for a change. It would've been much better with a pint though." He lifted his can to raise a toast.

"'Anyway, the shed wasn't going to stay like that. I ripped the window off the wall and used the wood for a nice little bonfire on November 5th. I bought a bucket of emulsion and painted it brown, inside and out. All fences and sheds should be painted brown. There should be law against painting anything outdoors in purple and yellow. All this new nonsense. I just don't understand it."

'Wilfred's wife was taken ill in 2016 and he looked after her until she died. I visited him often at his home and was shocked at how old and fragile my pal had become. Wilfred still talked about returning to his allotment on those rare occasions. He continued to pay the lease even though he couldn't tend to the garden regularly any more. The flowers died and the weeds started to take over the vegetable beds.

'Wilfred had quite a bad fall shortly after his wife passed away. He fell down the stairs after a few too many beers and broke his hip. "I tell you it was her. She pushed me down the stairs," he'd said when Pete visited him in hospital, pointing at the ceiling. "She never liked me drinking in the house."

'His son travelled up from Cornwall and thought it would be best for his father to sell the house and move into sheltered accommodation close to him. Going through his bank statements he cancelled the lease to the plot. By then everything above ground had grown out of control and the local kids used the grounds as a meeting point on the weekends. There had been other people looking at the allotment from time to time but they told Pete in passing that they didn't feel they had the energy to clear it up. Wilfred had died a few months ago.'

Finishing her story Inga took a sip from the glass of wine in her hand. 'If you ask me,' she said to her husband, 'an Iraqi uniform, a shed like a room out of *Arabian Night*s and a paper written in Arabic. It sounds to me that there is a connection.'

'You think so?' he asked sarcastically.

'There is no need for your sarcasm, Jonathan,' she replied, looking at him over the rim of her glasses. She used his Sunday name and he knew he was going to get into trouble if he carried on. Two weeks later there was a knock at the door.

'Hi, Inga, I have that translation you wanted.'

It felt like a minor miracle. Atif had come through for her for once. She smiled at him when he handed her a piece of paper.

'When I took it to our imam, he said there was a refugee from Iraq who comes for prayers every Friday so I gave it to him yesterday and he translated the readable part of it. I wrote it down for you and made you a list.'

Her eyes scanned over the events of the day in 1991.

'Thanks, Atif, tell April that we will have the kids on the weekend. I haven't seen them in a while and need my Nana fix.

'Strange,' she said as she closed the door and stepped back into the living room. 'There is nothing extraordinary about the events on that day in 1991 apart from this one right here. Did you ever hear anything about this?' Handing him the paper she pointed to the words halfway down the page. He took the note from her hands and began to read the short paragraph. Afterwards, he leaned back and looked at her.

'I'll be damned. Get us a cup of tea, will you, babe? I'll tell you a story about something that I haven't thought about in a very long time.'

'Go on, tell me now, I can't wait that long. You never volunteered anything about that war. The suspense is killing me.'

'Make me that tea first, love, and bring some biscuits too. It might take some time.'

23.

'How did I end up in this shithole of a country?' he asked himself yet again. Not only was it hot and dirty, it crawled with camel spiders, deadly snakes and scorpions. The smell of burning shit from the cesspits mingled with the stench of the decomposing camel they had discovered not far from their camp. How it died nobody knew but a family of desert foxes must have had a great feast. They found bones scattered all around, left for the vultures.

They were sweating like pigs during the day and shivering in their sleeping bags at night. There were frequent sandstorms and they could feel the sand permanently grinding on their teeth. They covered the bottom of their faces with scarfs and their eyes with goggles but the sand would always find a way in. It blurred their vision, settled in their ears and blocked their noses.

The oil wells had been burning for weeks and big black clouds of fumes turned day into night. When the wind blew in the wrong direction they got covered in specks of crude oil; they would find bits floating in their tea and taste it with every bite on their forks. It was like a glimpse through a window into hell.

They spent weeks preparing for this war and now it was over. It lasted one month, one week and four days. The ground assault started on the 24th of February and to everybody's surprise ended with a ceasefire one hundred hours later. He didn't fire a single shot. Not one. The only blood he saw being spilled was his own, when his wrench slipped and he cut his hand on a piece of metal.

The formidable Army of Republican Guards were surrendering in their droves and handing themselves over to the Allies. There had been a 'friendly fire' incident when two United States Air Force jets mistook two British armoured vehicles for Iraqi tanks and fired upon them, wounding many soldiers and killing nine. He had seen the carnage left behind when they recovered the tanks from the battlefield. To think there had been nine of his comrades inside made him angry and sad. Casualties of war. He loved his job but he was sadly reminded that war was not all about winning and glory. He thought of his wife and the wives who would never see their partners again, of the children who would grow up without them and of the parents left behind, never seeing their children grow old, never having grandchildren. He quickly put it to the back of his mind. Sentimentality didn't have a place on the battlefield. They had come here to do a job and they had done so with an extremely low casualty count, therefore in a way it had been very successful.

His unit had been given orders to clear the desert of debris. It was their task to bury the unrepairable vehicles in the sand. They had no contact with the outside world. Their unit had no radios therefore had little knowledge of the current situation. It was frustrating. He had been told that morning from a passing tank crew that although a lot of Republican Guards were surrendering their weapons, many had fled into the desert, hoping to avoid capture.

Even though they had agreed to a ceasefire and surrendered, these renegade soldiers remained a threat.

He had to stay vigilant and put the boys on guard once the sun went down. On a good day they were able to see for miles and would have spotted an approaching enemy from a distance but at night he wouldn't take any chances. He had taken the last shift. The sun had gone down and the temperature had dropped rapidly. He had slipped into his sleeping bag and taken shelter in his tent. It hardly deserved to be called a tent. It was a pane of camouflage plastic sheeting, draped over a piece of string held up by two sticks, but it was better than sleeping out in the open and it sheltered him from rain.

When the guard woke him from his slumber he was covered in dust. He felt constantly dirty and had dreamt of a long hot soak in his wife's bubble bath, surrounded by scented candles with a bottle of beer by his side. If the guys ever found out about this, there would be hell to pay and he would get ripped for it no end. The guard reported that everything had been quiet and all his men were now asleep in their preferred position on top of the tank.

The night was dark. That sounded funny when he wrote it down in a letter to his wife but the darkness was different in the desert. With no civilisation around them there was hardly any light apart from the moon and the millions of stars above, well, when he could see the sky before the oilfields were set alight. He tried to describe the beauty of it to his wife once but words failed him. There was no sound either apart from his men's snoring. At times it felt like being in a vacuum, void of sight and sound.

'If it weren't for the smell of that camel,' he thought. They will have to bury the rest of that thing at first light. He wouldn't be able to eat his breakfast with the stench up his nostrils. He boiled some water for a cup of tea on his little firepit and wished he had some of the cake left his wife had sent him for Valentine's Day. The cake was long gone. Shared and demolished on the day it arrived.

A noise, just the faintest sound, made him sit up and listen, holding his breath he turned his head left and right.

Slowly he reached for his sub-machine gun lying at the side next to him, and lifted it over his shoulder. He felt for his pistol in its holster and picked up his night vision goggles. His tent stood behind a small ridge he had thrown up with the digger. He hoped the ridge would shelter him from the wind and most of the smell from the camel. He stood up and made his way in the direction he thought the noise originated from. Approaching the little ridge, he crouched close to the ground and was careful not to make any noise.

There it was again. Closer this time.

He lifted the gun of his shoulder and switched his night vision goggles on. The landscape in front of him turned green in an instant. He looked to the left. There was a desert fox. Through the green light of his night vision goggles he saw its eyes shining brightly in the night. He sighed, only a fox. The tension started to leave his body, when to the right this time, he heard the noise again. 'Fuck.' His head swung around, weapon pointing in that direction, ready to fire. A second desert fox, startled by his appearance, retreated to a safe distance.

He slowly started to release the breath he didn't realise he was holding and cursed the creature. How stupid to become so agitated by the sound of two harmless foxes. What were they doing here? Would they not be better off, feeding from the carcass of the camel close by? Sensing no danger from him, the fox slowly made its way back into his field of vision. He scanned the area. Just about a metre from the fox he could see a bundle on the floor. Whatever it was, the fox clearly had shown an interest in it.

It could be nothing but, remembering the story of scores of retreating Iraqis into the desert, it could easily be an IED (improvised explosive device) left to kill and maim anybody close by. They had buried the bodies of some soldiers from a burnt-out tank that afternoon and checked the area for survivors. He was certain that there was nobody left alive. They were going to dig a hole for the tank in the morning. Since the foxes hadn't blown up, he was certain that the bundle was not triggered by motion. It was still risky but he decided to have a closer look.

Slowly he moved towards the bundle, gun at the ready. All the way there he waited for a remote detonation that would blow him to kingdom come and make his wife a widow, his child fatherless. Every muscle in his body was tense. Nothing happened and nobody took a shot at him. Staring at the bundle for what seemed like an eternity, he removed the goggles and decided to check it out. He reached for his torch, which was attached to his belt, switched it on and shone it over the blanket. There were no visible wires sticking out so he peeled back the edge of the sheet with his weapon.

The bundle was not an explosive. It was a baby.

It couldn't have been much older than a few hours, maybe a day, there was no way of knowing for sure. He looked around and shone the torch over the ground nearby for any signs of its mother. Where was she? What had happened to her? He couldn't see a body. He crouched down on his knees. The fox must have come for an easy meal. Fresher than the camel anyhow.

At first, he thought the baby was dead but then he heard a faint whimper. He didn't know what to do with it and was in two minds to just walk away and leave it where he found it. The fox would put it out of its misery. The baby was destined to die anyway, it was hardly alive as it was. One more casualty of war. He was a soldier, not a humanitarian. These things happen. All these thoughts rushed through his mind at speed but then he thought of his own child at home, safe with her mother and the difficult birth his wife had to endure. She had been fortunate to have had an incubator and a full medical team on standby. This poor creature had nothing, maybe not even a few more hours to live. Even he couldn't be so cruel.

He picked the little bundle off the dusty ground and put his mouth next to its ear. 'There is no harm in giving you comfort for the next few hours is there, little one?' he whispered. Returning to his tent, he got a spoon from his canteen and started feeding the infant water from the pot he had boiled for his tea. 'If you survive till the morning, I will take you to the British field hospital,' he said to the child. 'Then you are on your own, kid.'

He was beginning to nod off looking at the child in his lap. At first, he thought it had died in the night but when he pulled the blanket from its head, two beautiful dark eyes were trying to focus on his face. He boiled some more water and took the baby to show to the lads nearby.

'Look what I found in the night, lads.' He held the baby up and showed it to his men. They were oooing and aaaaing, passing it round from man to man. He recalled having the same reaction from them when he showed off the little desert mouse, he captured in their Portakabin back in Al Jubail.

'Needs changing, mate,' one of his men said holding the baby as far away from him without dropping it. The baby was handed back to him in a hurry since he was the only 'daddy' in the troop and knew what he was supposed to do.

'All yours, I'll make breakfast,' his mate said and he started to collect the ration packs with 'breakfast' written on the front.

'Na, Dave, first job this morning before you are even allowed to think about having breakfast, is to bury that stinking camel out there. Nobody is having anything to eat till that is done. That smell is making me sick.'

Dave didn't argue with him and mounted the digger moments later. Jonathan carried the baby back to his tent.

The baby was a girl and her back was covered in black tar-like paste. He cleaned her up as well as he could. He couldn't remember doing that for his own daughter but then again, his daughter had been in an incubator for four days and had been looked after by the paediatric nurses.

He discovered that the umbilical cord had just been cut but not wound. He didn't know whether it was too late in the day but he tied a cord around it at the bottom. He changed her and made a nappy out of bandages in his emergency pack. Then he wrapped her back up in one of his cleaner T-shirts. He fed her more water from a spoon and after he had his own breakfast, without the smell of dead camel, he was ready to take her to the field hospital.

'Won't be long lads.' He sped off with the child in the footwell of his Land Rover.

It didn't take him long to drive the few miles to the army medical station where he had his arm lanced a while ago. He handed the little girl over to the nurses and told them about his discovery. He left the tent, promising a full report. He was glad that it was over. He had done his job. He had taken one casualty of war and had handed her over to the authorities. They would know what to do.

24.

Hakim had pulled the cart through the desert for three days. He was exhausted and could feel the strength leaving his body with every step he took. Throwing caution to the wind he walked through the day, if they were discovered, so be it. *Inshallah*.

He came close a few times to laying down next to her and waiting for things to come but somehow his will to survive was greater. Nazreen was still out of it, delirious with fever, in and out of consciousness. It was a blessing in disguise; he couldn't find the words to tell her that she'd lost her daughter. He cleaned the afterbirth and thought that finally the bleeding had stopped. They were running out of water and needed a place to regain their strength. The thought of her dying out here in the desert, after all he had endured, kept him on his feet. They were travelling north and the landscape was changing from a muddy grey to a muddy brown. He hoped that they were going to come across some villages soon, before he would collapse from exhaustion. He rationed his water intake, so she could drink but still he watched her getting weaker and weaker.

For the first time since he had been drafted into the army, he felt remorse. For the first time he thought about the men he had killed in battle, the men he had sentenced to death. He remembered the face of her father before he sent him to his execution. He wondered if his face showed the same despair and hopelessness. All those men left someone behind who would grieve for them. This time he was going to be the one left behind and the thought of it made him shiver. He was terrified. He sat down next to her on the cart.

'I am not going to share their fate, Nazreen.' He looked at her face and longed for her to open her eyes. 'If you die, I will die with you, do you hear me, Nazreen? We are going to die together. I can't carry on if you are not in this world. Please, you need to hang on. For me!' He climbed off the cart and continued their journey north.

When he thought he could not take another step, he saw a fire glowing in the distance. He was jubilant and didn't care whether it was friend or enemy. Finding the strength from within he slowly covered the distance and collapsed outside the camp. Hands helped him up and carried him near a fire, friendly faces invited him to drink from a bowl and he gulped the hot liquid that tasted as sweet as any honey he'd ever had.

'We have been blessed,' he said to the man holding the bowl to his mouth. 'Allah has not abandoned us.

'Nazreen,' was the last word he uttered pointing to the cart before he closed his eyes.

He woke up in a tent after what he thought must have been days. The Bedouins who had rescued them were on their way home. They had set up camp because of an approaching sandstorm. Listening to the wind howling around the tent outside, he felt lucky. The sandstorm would certainly have finished them out there. He looked around. The men were sat on a Persian rug around a shisha. They leaned against big cushions, talking quietly to one another so as not to disturb his sleep. Sheep were tied to a pole in a corner, munching on their feed. When the man nearest to him saw that he was awake he handed him a bowl with stew and Hakim thought he'd never eaten anything as wonderful in his entire life.

'Nazreen?' he asked, taking a big sip of sheep's milk somebody handed him.

'The women have taken your wife into their tent. They are looking after her. You don't need to worry. Rest now and recover your strength. We are going to stay till the wind dies down.'

He was grateful that Allah had been merciful and sent him the Bedouins. They were finally safe, they were going to live. Hakim thanked the man in front of him and closed his eyes. When he opened them for the second time, he felt he had gathered enough strength to get up and talk to the men. He walked over to the fire on unsteady legs and they helped him to sit down. Naturally the conversation soon turned to the turmoil their country was in.

'Have you seen any of the fighting?' he asked. 'We escaped from Basra before the fighting began and then my wife fell ill. We walked for days. I don't even know where we are.'

The man next to him took in a deep breath of the pipe and released a big cloud of perfumed smoke into the air. He shook his head.

'We haven't seen much of the war. We saw the rockets and the planes fly over our tents but that is all. We don't know what happened and we don't really care who won. To us it doesn't matter who is in charge. Never has been and never will. We are our own masters and we will go wherever we please. That is the ancient way and it will be the way for generations to come. We are not frightened of anybody.'

The wind died down and he ventured outside for the first time in days. He inquired about Nazreen's health at the entrance to the women's tent and was told that the fever had broken but that she was still very weak; she was sleeping now.

'When she woke up the last time she asked about her baby. We didn't find a baby in the cart. It was only the woman. Can you tell me what happened?' He told her that the baby had died shortly after birth and that he buried it in the desert. The woman nodded.

'I will be as gentle as I can,' she said and stepped back into the tent. A short while later he heard Nazreen cry out in pain. It broke his heart and he wanted to run into the tent to comfort her but he knew that he wasn't allowed. He walked away from the tents, first it was slowly but soon he ran into the desert and sat behind a boulder. There he started to cry quietly into the palms of his hands.

25.

The Bedouins stayed another night and Hakim enjoyed the comfort and hospitality. That night he was told that they had to continue their journey west the next day. In the morning they packed up the tents and saddled their camels. They left him with two waterskins and with as much food as they could spare. Before the tribe set off on their journey Hakim was told that if he continued to go northeast for a couple of days, he would reach the banks of the Euphrates.

They had stayed for a few more days after the Bedouins left. Nazreen slept a lot but when she was awake her gaze followed him with accusing eyes. She didn't want to talk. Every time he tried to speak to her, she turned her head in the opposite direction. He wanted to explain that he had no choice; the baby had died, it wasn't his fault. They both nearly died too. Still it didn't seem to be enough that he had saved her life.

She was getting stronger every day and able to sit up but she hadn't found the strength yet to stand on her own two feet. In the end he couldn't wait any longer and he lifted her into the back of the cart. They continued their journey in silence. That night by the fire she turned her face to him for the first time.

'Tell me about my baby,' she said quietly.

Relieved that she decided to make the first step, he moved closer to her and took her hand. He dared to pull her hand to his lips and placed a kiss on the back of her hand, looking into her eyes.

'I ask for your forgiveness, *Habibi,*' he said sincerely. 'She was the most beautiful baby I have ever seen. She looked so tiny in my hands and had the fullest head of hair. It was as black as yours. I am so sorry. I sent a prayer to Allah and asked for his mercy. I tried everything in my power to keep her alive but Allah in his wisdom took her to paradise. She died in my arms; it was His will.

'I wrapped her in the blanket you showed me and I put the little bracelet round her wrist. I laid her body next to yours so you would know how much she loved you but you didn't wake up. Instead, you were slipping away from me and I couldn't wait any longer. You would have died too, Nazreen. I had to bury her as the Prophet demands.'

Silent tears were running down her face and he folded her into his embrace.

'You should have let me die with her, Hakim.' She looked up at his face and he saw that she meant every word. 'My heart broke when Aliyah told me she had died. They had to restrain me from killing myself. You should have let me die there and then.' He felt as helpless then as he did that night and hugged her body closer.

'Never,' he said passionately. 'As Allah is my witness, I could not live without you. I am so, so sorry,' he repeated and stroked her back, trying to comfort her sobs.

Suddenly he remembered. 'I got this.' He let go of her body and reached into the cart for his satchel. He pulled out a little piece of cloth and handed it to her.

'I told her that her mother will never forget her.'

She received the cloth with trembling fingers and unfolded it. It was a tiny lock of jet-black hair. She clutched the little lock to her heart and looked at him, her eyes shining wet with tears. She knew that it was not customary to keep such things and it made his gesture heartfelt and precious.

'Thank you,' she said, folding the little lock back in the cloth. 'I will not forget your kindness.'

He sat back next to her and put an arm around her shoulders. Nobody was around to see, so he kissed her gently on her forehead.

'Sleep now, you are safe here with me,' he said quietly and after a while he heard her deep breathing. He settled down opposite her and fell asleep with a smile.

The following days and against his wishes, she insisted on walking for short distances. She only climbed back into the cart when she felt tired and couldn't walk any longer. She had been lying on her back long enough. Soon she was well on the road to recovery. It might have taken two days for the Bedouins to walk the distance they described but it took a lot longer than two days for them. They were running out of water and food. They had seen few signs that made them believe they were getting closer to the river. He was unsure they were going in the right direction at all, till, one morning, he spotted green bushes and palm trees appearing in the distance. The ground they walked on became smoother, more even, and finally the Euphrates appeared before them, winding its way to the south.

With a triumphant cry she ran past him into the water and submersed herself in it. She jumped around like a little child and her enthusiasm soon caught on. He dived in after her and soon they splashed water at each other, laughing like lunatics. Then they both lay on the riverbank, trying to catch their breath. He sat up and discovered a small boat on the other side of the shores, hidden in the reeds. He swam over and by the time he returned her clothes had dried in the sun. They transferred their belongings into the boat, leaving the battered cart behind.

Hakim rowed further upstream. Finding the boat had given him confidence that there was a village close by. If not, there must be a house where they would be able to buy provisions and hear of much-needed news. They saw the outskirts of a town around the next bend in the river and he left Nazreen behind with the boat. When he returned he had a sack full of fresh fruit and vegetables, flour and fresh meat. She clapped her hands in excitement. Tonight, they would feast. After they polished every bit of meat from the bones they lay around the fire, sharing the figs he bought.

'I was surprised to hear that Saddam hasn't been chased back to Baghdad. The infidels declared a ceasefire shortly after they bombed Highway 80.'

He saw her shiver when he reminded her of that frightful night.

'They say that thousands of people died in their vehicles and at the side of the road. I guess the Americans thought they did enough by chasing us out of Kuwait. Maybe they even hoped that the Iraqi people would start a revolution on their own. How wrong they were, Nazreen. Did they really think that the thought of freedom was greater than the fear of Saddam?

'I spoke to a man who told me that there was fierce fighting in Basra. He fled for his life from the rebels. The government regained control but he's still not willing to go back because nobody is safe.

'He heard that Saddam's Republican Guards rounded the people up in the square and killed everybody who was suspected to have had a hand in the uprising. The Americans denied Saddam from flying planes in Iraq but they allowed him to fly his armed helicopters. The infidels are all idiots.' He shook his head. 'The Americans didn't come to the aid of the Marsh Arabs either when they started bombing the islands. There was no revolution left and still nobody came to their rescue, thousands of people were killed. Men, women and children. How could they leave him alive? I'm ashamed I ever wore the uniform.

'I hate him, Nazreen. He ruined my life.' Hakim put another couple of branches onto the fire and sat in silence. She left him alone to be with his thoughts and washed the pans in the river.

Saddam was still in charge but all was not lost. Nobody knew he was a deserter and he intended to put his uniform to good use. Further north along the river, he hoped the support for the government would be as strong as ever and nobody was going to question him. He knew that his uniform was as good as a note from the Devil himself.

He had no doubt that from there they would make it to the border. He couldn't stay. For the time being, he would travel in the thobe the Bedouins had given him and tell Nazreen to stay out of sight. That was his plan. When she returned from the river he was in a better mood.

He only changed into his uniform once more to confiscate a boat with a sail and a small engine in one of the villages further upstream. He told Nazreen that he had paid for it in exchange for their smaller boat. He had changed back into his other clothes by then and looked like an ordinary fisherman. Nazreen didn't listen to his explanation; she was just happy for him to be back.

26.

From afar the boat looked like any other boat on the river. Hakim set the sail to save petrol and they were gliding through the water almost silently. Little waves splashed against the side of the boat and she dipped her hand in and out, running the cool liquid through her fingers.

They sailed past palm trees and reeds on the embankments on both sides. The houses, rectangular like shoeboxes, looked deserted when they sailed past. All the shutters were closed to shield the inhabitants from the blazing sun. The land was fertile near the riverbank and sheep and goats were grazing peacefully in the fields, seeking shelter underneath the trees when it got too hot.

White birds, their feathers glistening like snow, were asleep on one leg and cranes were stalking amongst the reeds looking for fish. She waved at the children playing on the jetties as they jumped high in the air and landed with a splash in the water. Further away from the villages it turned quiet once again.

'Isn't it beautiful and peaceful here, Hakim?' she said, glancing over her shoulder to look at him.

'It sure is, *Habibi*,' he said smiling.

For the first time since they had left the desert behind, she saw him with different eyes. He was just as handsome as she remembered him all those years ago but he had grown from a boy into a man. He was tall with dark hair and the fashionable moustache that she saw on him the first day had grown into a beard. 'He didn't have a single hair on his face when he held my hand the day he declared his love for me,' she thought and wondered if the hairs would tickle her nose if he kissed her.

She scolded herself for having those thoughts. She was still married after all and although it was all right for a man to have more than one wife, providing the first wife didn't include a clause prohibiting it in their marriage contract, it wasn't allowed the other way around. How unfair she thought. Her eyes went back to Hakim.

The hands that were holding the rudder with a firm grip were big and strong. She knew they could be gentle. She still felt his fingers on her face. They left a warm glow behind in her heart when he stroked her cheek and put a strand of her hair back under the hijab earlier. His arms were powerful; she felt his muscles every time he had to carry her but she knew they could be tender when she was enveloped in them. His eyes were hazel and had little specks of gold when he laughed. Yesterday she pretended to be asleep on the riverbank when they stopped for a break but she had watched him take his tunic off to wash. She had seen his muscular body, droplets of water running down the back of his spine. When his fringe fell into his eyes and he pushed his hair back with one hand, he looked almost fifteen again.

He put his uniform on the previous day and for a moment he turned back into the frightful monster she had seen on that first day he came back into her life. His eyes had turned dark, cold and empty. She wondered what he had seen and done to become like that. When he came back with the boat and discarded his uniform, he also changed back into the person she remembered. 'Just like the story I was told by my mother about the man who was possessed by an evil jinni,' she thought.

'How much further do you think we have to travel?' she asked from her spot at the front of the boat.

'I don't think it will be much longer now.' He corrected the course of the boat to avoid a sandbank. 'We will make camp a little further upstream tonight so you can stretch your legs.' She gave him a thankful smile.

When the sun was setting, he sailed the boat close to the riverbank and they set up camp. He felt safe and lit a fire. She prepared the fish he had caught earlier. She put the fish on sticks and it was cooking above the fire, which sent a warm glow across her body. He approached the subject of a new life almost every day they had travelled on the river, but she was reluctant to even talk about it.

'How can I leave the country of my birth, Hakim?' she said and handed him the fish. 'I am still married. You said Mohamed was going to find me once the war was over.' He didn't see the pain on her face, she had already turned her head.

He looked at her across the fire and braced himself for what he was about to say. 'I don't think there is a chance he survived the attack on the airbase, *Habibi*.

'You saw the fires of the bombs with your own eyes. There is no way he could have survived. When I left Mohamed, he was in a room at the front of the building. I am sorry.'

'But he might have survived.' She stared at her hands holding the plate and seeing her concern for Mohamed cut Hakim like a knife.

'He's dead,' he said more harshly than he intended. 'So are all the people on the road to Basra and the people in the marshes, Nazreen. So is your baby.' She winced and he knew he was deliberately cruel. He looked at her and moved closer to where she sat, staring into the fire. He took her plate and put it to one side. He lifted her chin till she met his eyes.

'It was Allah's will.' She moved away from him with fear in her eyes.

'No, Hakim. No. You don't know what he's like. He's a monster and if he survived, he will come for me. He will not rest till he finds me and this time he's going to kill me for sure. Look what he's done to me!' She lifted her dress and turned around.

'Do you see these scars, Hakim?' she screamed at him. She pointed to the large burn on the back of her thigh. 'This I got when I stood on his foot by accident.' She turned around further and he could see the ugly red streaks on her back, left behind by a belt. 'These scars are left from the time I didn't make his tea the way he wanted it.' She pulled up her sleeves and exposed horrible cigarette burn marks on the top of her arms. 'I have a story for every blemish on my body.' She turned back to him, dropping her dress back to the floor.

'Can you imagine what he will do to me when he finds out I lost the baby?'

Her eyes filled with tears. He rushed to her and hugged her tightly, letting her cry for her mother and father, her child and all the other victims of a war that nobody would remember. Exhausted she stepped out of his embrace and sat on the floor.

'He was a bad man, Hakim. I will never be rid of him till he or I are dead,' she said staring into the fire. Hakim looked down on her in silence for a long time.

'He's dead, *Habibi*.' He paused. 'I killed him.'

She lifted her head and her eyes widened. It was unusually hard for him to look her in the eyes and confess to his crime so he started walking up and down in front of her.

'When I talked to him after the arrest, he tried to bribe me. First it was money. Then he offered you to me as a gift, to do with you "whatever I please", so I shot him. I came to you straight after.' He looked at her.

'I don't regret killing him,' he said stubbornly. 'I regret that I haven't been there for you earlier.'

She was shocked. Not by the fact that he shot her husband. She knew of the demon who lived inside of him when he wore the uniform. She was shocked to hear that she was finally free. Mohamed was never going to hurt her again.

'He will never hurt you again,' Hakim said, echoing the words from inside her head. 'Are you all right, *Habibi*?' He sat down next to her, anxiously waiting for her to speak.

'I'm glad he's dead,' she said quietly after a while and squeezed his fingers. She gathered her blanket around her, laid back and closed her eyes. He sat looking at her for a little while longer.

'I will be the man she deserves,' he said to himself before he fell asleep next to her.

The next days they spent sailing up the river. They had run out of petrol for the engine but luckily the wind was blowing in the right direction. She sat at her favourite spot at the front of the boat, her long hair flying like a flag in the breeze. Her face had changed after the night he confessed to her husband's murder. It showed her newfound freedom and he liked it. Before, she looked like a middle-aged woman, hunched over by the harshness of her life. Now she looked tall, young and vibrant, full of life.

'There is no future for this country under Saddam's tyranny,' he said one day. 'I thought the infidels would dispose of him and we could have raised our country back from the ashes.

'Now, nothing is going to change and it will only get worse. They will hear of my desertion and they will come looking for me. They will kill me, Nazreen.'

She didn't doubt his words. If they were discovered, she was sure that they would execute him on the spot. She wasn't afraid to die next to him. She was frightened they wouldn't kill her and violated her, till she died of her injuries or shame. She shuddered at the thought. Her whole family had perished one way or another. Hakim was right. There was nothing left to live for in this country.

'Well,' she said with a smile. 'We'd better pray to Allah they don't then.'

27.

As the month changed from April into May the weather changed too and the temperature climbed higher every day. They slept, hidden in the reeds under the sail, sheltered from the sun and travelled at night when there was less traffic on the river. They would soon reach what he thought were the outskirts of Al-Hindiyah near Karbala.

'I'm going to stretch my legs for a bit,' he said to her, leaving her to doze a little while longer. She was busy getting the sail ready when he returned.

'I found a hut not far from here, Nazreen. Would you like to stay on dry land for a bit? It looks like rain. Look at the colour of the sky over there.'

She turned her head in the direction he pointed at. She didn't fancy getting wet so soon after she woke up and they took shelter in the deserted hut on the banks of the river. The owners must have left in a hurry or they were taken by surprise. The door was unlocked and pots and pans were strewn all over. There were shards of broken dishes and remains of food decaying around a fire. What had happened here? She cleared the floor with a broom she discovered in a corner and they shared the last of the cold fish she'd caught that morning.

It was turning dark when he got up and with a glance in her direction pulled the uniform out of his bag. Instantly, he was transformed back into the man he was before. She shrank away from him as he turned around to say goodbye. It made him feel shameful to see the terror in her eyes.

'Don't be frightened, my love,' he pleaded with her. 'I promise I will never wear it again; I will burn it once we are safe.' He pulled out the gun and inspected it, which frightened her even more.

'Where are you going?' she asked. 'Please don't leave me on my own.'

'I have to, *Habibi*. I'm sorry. I need to find out if we are going to be safe if we stay on the river. I'll be as quick as I can.'

'Can I not come with you? I'm frightened you won't come back and that I will never see you again.'

He took her in his arms and laughed. 'Don't be silly.' He kissed her quickly on her forehead. 'I will always come back for you,' he said. 'I promise. I must go on my own. It's not safe for you out there and don't light a fire till I get back.'

He opened the door and looked back over his shoulder at her, smiling. He almost couldn't leave. She looked so vulnerable, standing there, small and alone in the middle of the room. He tore himself away. 'I won't be long,' he said and left.

He marched down the path that would hopefully lead him to the houses outside of town and knocked on the gate of the first house he saw. A pair of eyes peeked through a gap in the fence taking in his appearance, deliberating whether he could be trusted. He could hear a commotion. People were scuffling about behind the gate. He heard a nail being driven into a wall and mumbled voices debated what to do next.

'I come in peace,' he softly shouted in the direction of the people inside.

A man opened the gate leaving a small gap, looking him up and down. After a minute of contemplating the man opened the gate fully.

'*As-salaam-alaikum*,' Hakim greeted the man.

'*Wa-alaikum-salaam*,' replied the man and gestured him to enter. He was led into a small courtyard.

'We broke down two miles down the road. I've sent my driver into town to find a mechanic but he's been gone for two hours and hasn't come back yet. We have no food or water. Could I ask for a drink, *sadeeqi?*'

'Please sit,' said the man and pointed at the rug that was placed under a tree in the middle of the yard. Cushions were scattered all around in a circle. It looked like he interrupted a game of backgammon.

A small transistor radio played quietly in the corner. Hakim looked around and his eyes fell on the picture of Saddam on the wall. It looked askew and out of place in the otherwise empty courtyard. The man called his wife to fetch some tea and soon there was a selection of nuts, olives and flatbread. She silently placed a cup of mint tea in front of him and disappeared back into the shadows under the arches.

'You are alone? her husband asked. 'I didn't know what to think when you knocked on the gate. Can you bring me news of my son? He works as a porter in the hospital. My son hasn't come back and we have no news of him.' Hakim shook his head.

'We've heard terrible stories from my daughter-in-law. She managed to flee the city of Karbala and came here. For the first couple of days it looked like the rebels were winning but the government forces were too powerful. I ask you, how is it possible to fly helicopter gunships in a no-fly zone? They saw tanks with big signs saying, *No more Shia after today*. She said that patients were thrown out of hospital windows and doctors and nurses who helped the injured rebels were taken away. Young men were arrested and taken to the stadium. I need to know if Ali is alive. Can you find out for me? I'm too frail to go and I'm too old to look after so many people.'

'How many grandchildren have you got?' Hakim asked.

'I have five. All boys, *mashallah*. The oldest is twelve, the youngest four months. Can you help me find my boy?'

'I'm sorry,' Hakim said. 'I'm not going in that direction but I'm sure that your son will return soon now the city is back under government control.'

The old man watched Hakim look at Saddam's picture, hanging limp off the nail on the wall. Hakim was somehow sure that the son fought for the rebels and was probably dead.

'Is it true that they still haven't extinguished the fires on the oilfields?' the old man asked, changing the subject, as he poured some more tea from the pot.

'I think you know more about the oil-fields than I,' Hakim replied. 'I've been out in the desert and haven't seen a newspaper in months.'

'Please be my guest.' He pointed at a newspaper on top of a bookcase under the arches and called his wife to fetch it for him. 'It's not a recent one, I'm afraid. It's probably a month old but there is an article about the fires in Kuwait. The Americans were struggling to put them out.' He handed the paper to Hakim.

'It's going to rain soon,' the old man said, lifting his head and sucking in the scent like an animal. 'I can smell the moisture in the air.

Very unusual for this time of year, you know. I am seventy-four years old and I never witnessed rain in July. Very unusual indeed.' He sat back.

The paper was from March. Hakim scanned through the pages and suddenly stopped. He took a sharp breath. He asked if he could tear the page out of the paper and the old man nodded in surprise. Hakim folded the page and stuffed it in the breast pocket of his jacket. He looked at his watch, thanked the man for his hospitality and told him that it was time for him to go.

'I will enquire about your son and send a message,' he said stepping back onto the street. 'May Allah bless Saddam Hussein,' the old man shouted as an afterthought as he shut the gate but Hakim didn't reply. He slowly walked away from the house, trying to make sense of the words he had just read.

Impossible, Nazreen would never forgive him.

28.

He could see the hut in the distance even through the rain. There was light shining through the gaps in the shutters that he'd closed before he left. He told her not to make a fire or light the lamp they found hanging from the ceiling. Why had she ignored him? It was too dangerous for a woman to be out here on her own, he told her so. Anger welled up in him and he fell into a trot.

As he turned around the last bend the building appeared in full view. Two horses, illuminated by the light streaming out of the open entrance, were grazing on a patch in front of the hut. He heard loud jeering and then he heard Nazreen scream.

'No, Allah, no!' He started to run towards the house, reaching for his gun. He stumbled and fell. Jumping back to his feet he finally managed to pull his gun from its holster.

A thousand pictures flashed through his head as he hurried towards the hut. His blood started to rush through his veins as he imagined what he was going to find. He stormed into the house, gun in hand, with a war cry he had practised on the battlefields of Iran. One man in plain clothes stood opposite the entrance, watching the two people wrestling on the floor, laughing and spurring the man on to finish the job so he could take his turn. Hakim shot him without any hesitation.

The man clutched a hand to his chest. One more shot and the bullet blew his head apart. It made a sound like a watermelon dropping on the floor, leaving blood, bones and bits of brain splattered all over the back of the wall right up to the ceiling. The man fell to the floor like a sack of potatoes, dropping his rifle. The other assailant, his pants still around his ankles, tried to get to his feet, but it was too late. Hakim kicked him off Nazreen, who tried frantically to get away, pushing herself backwards into a corner.

The man tried to crawl towards the Kalashnikov his pal had dropped on the floor. Hakim kicked the gun away, grabbed him by the back of his hair and slammed his head into the ground over and over, till he stopped moving. Panting, Hakim rose to his feet and shot the man through the back of his head. He turned around, gun in hand, expecting more men. There was no one. He turned back and hurried over to where she cowered in the corner.

'Nazreen!' He stood in front of her. She put both hands in front of her body, palms up and threw herself at his feet, kissing his boots and begging him for mercy. He pulled her shaking body up into his arms. She shrieked and immediately started to fight. Furiously she lashed out at him with her fingers curled into claws, scratching him deeply on his cheek.

'It's me Nazreen. Look at me!' He firmly grabbed her by her arms. '*Habibi*, it's me, Hakim!' But she didn't seem to hear him. Her eyes were squeezed shut. She continued to fight him like a fury, trying to headbutt him, her knees trying to connect with his groin all the while screaming at him to let her go. He let go of one arm and slapped her across the face, regretting it in an instant. But she stopped.

Her body went limp. He pulled her back into his embrace. 'I'm so, so sorry,' he said. He put one arm under her knees and picked her up. 'Close your eyes,' he said, stepping over the body in front of him. 'Don't look.' He carried her outside and gently lowered her to the ground next to the horses.

'Stay here and don't move, my love. I will be back shortly.' She grabbed hold of his uniform and he had to prise her hands from his sleeve; they were cold as ice. She didn't speak, just looked at him in shock.

'I won't go far, darling. I will just have a look at the men inside, then I will be right back.' He saw that one of her eyelids was starting to swell and she had a gash on the bridge of her nose. He looked into her eyes. 'You let me down again,' they seemed to say and she was right. He promised her she would be safe with him and he failed her again but he swore that it was never going to happen again, ever, not while he had a breath in his body.

He left her sobbing quietly into her gown and entered the hut. He searched the men for clues. 'They are Mukhabarat, I'm sure,' he said into the empty room.

'Now they are dead Mukhabarat,' a voice said quietly behind him.

He turned around, startled. Nazreen stood behind him, her face still streaked from tears but she had a defiant look on her face. She walked past him till she stood next to the dead body of the man who tried to rape her earlier. She turned him over with her foot. The left side of his face was almost gone. The bullet had left a big gap in his skull. Half of his forehead was missing and she saw grey brain matter speckled with fragments of teeth and bone, mixed together with sand and blood on the floor next to his face. The force of the bullet had dislodged the remaining eye. It seemed to be staring at her, dangling down his cheek by the optic nerve still attached to the socket. She spat into the remainder of his face.

'This is for every man, woman and child you have ever hurt, you bastard,' she hissed. 'I am never going to be frightened or used by a man again.' She straightened her back and holding her head high she left the room. He joined her once he had extinguished the lamp.

'We have to go and we have to go now, Nazreen. People will come looking for these men once it gets light. These guys will have had orders from somebody and I don't want to be anywhere near this place when they come.' She nodded.

'I heard them arrive outside the hut about an hour after you left. It was dark by then but I didn't light a fire, just like you told me. I heard one of them laugh and boast about what he had done to the people last time he was here. I thought they would pass by but just then it started to rain. I sat behind the door, hoping they'd think it was locked but they kicked it hard. It flew from its hinges and buried me underneath. They pulled me out from under it and the first man punched me in the face so hard I fell to the floor. When I came round he was on me, holding my mouth shut with one hand and pushing my dress up with the other. I bit his hand and screamed. It was lucky you returned when you did. A few minutes later and he...' She stopped in midsentence and shuddered. He put an arm around her shoulders, hoping to give her comfort.

'It will never happen again, I swear. From now on I will never let you out of my sight again.' She looked up at him through her eyelashes and he saw the struggle inside of her whether to believe him or not.

'Let's put it behind us and go back to the boat,' he said. She got up and stretched out her hand, pulling him up till he stood in front of her.

'You've saved my life twice now, Hakim. There was nothing but pain and suffering before you came back into my life. I am glad you found me and I will go anywhere you want me to. I believe in you and I believe you will never leave me behind again.'

With that she lifted herself up on her tiptoes and kissed him lightly on his cheek. 'I think we should put the men in the boat and send them downstream,' she suggested. 'We take their horses. They are going to be more useful in the mountains anyway, if that's where we are going.'

Hakim could not believe how resilient she had become. Standing in front of him she looked like a completely different person. Before tonight she appeared to be timid and frightened but now she looked tall and strong. He could still feel her lips on his cheek where she kissed him and he knew one thing for sure.

Nazreen was never going to find out that her baby had survived.

29.

Inga looked at her husband in stunned silence.

'It was you, wasn't it?' She jumped to her feet but he said nothing. 'It WAS you! Why on God's earth have you never told me about that, Jon?' She shook her head in disbelief.

'My husband the hero,' she exclaimed proudly and gave him a big hug. 'I think this deserves a medal, love.'

'It was nothing.' She looked at him in bewilderment.

'I beg to differ, my love. How can you say it was nothing? You saved a little girl's life. If anyone deserves a medal it should be you. Nothing, my arse. It's all right for the Beckhams of the world to receive their OBE but you think you don't deserve a medal? You're weird. A real hero should be recognised for exactly that.

'You saved a little girl's life!' she started to repeat herself.

'It wasn't as heroic as you might think, Inga,' he said.

'I have a slightly different opinion what qualifies a hero. A hero is a soldier who under sniper attack still rescues his comrade who's lying wounded in the street. A hero holds a position to defend his comrades by himself, till help arrives.' He shrugged his shoulders.

'Heroic is being shot through the head by a sniper, making it back from the brink of death and carrying on with life, although you're nearly blind.' She knew he was referring to his friend Simon Brown. 'I found a baby in the desert and delivered it to the nearest medical facility. There was nothing heroic about that, love. Anyway, it wasn't a big deal. I didn't pick her up because I felt it was my duty. I thought the baby would not survive the night and felt she shouldn't die alone. I felt sorry for her. Hell, I don't even know if she's alive now. I returned to the boys and we carried on with our job. I'd forgotten all about that night, that's how unimportant it was in the scheme of things. I'm no hero. Let's forget about it. I don't want any fuss.'

'No, no, no, no. No. Out of the question. If you wanted it to remain a secret you should have kept the story to yourself and pleaded ignorance.

I think you're a proper hero even if you don't. I'm so proud of you, babe. Something good has come out of that shitty war after all. Anyway, if that uniform is connected to the baby you found, it means that person knows something and we have an ex-Republican Guard living in the neighbourhood.

'To leave a baby in the desert to die. What sort of a human being does that? It's plain nasty. Poor defenceless little creature. You might not be interested in being a hero but I'm damned if I'm not the proud wife of one. I can't wait to tell Libby. She'll be so proud of you,' and she reached for the phone.

'But first I am going to speak to the nitwit who wrote about the "body" in the first place. Let's see if people still snigger behind our backs then.'

'Nobody sniggered behind anybody's back, love. It's all in your head.' She ignored his comment and continued to search for the number of the paper on her phone.

He knew that once she had a bee in her bonnet there was no stopping her and he just had to ride the wave. 'Wait,' he demanded in a stern voice, which made her stop punching the numbers into the pad.

'Before you go and tell the whole world I have something to show you. Without it you will sound like an attention-seeking madwoman with too much imagination.'

He climbed the stairs before she could reply and opened to door to his office. He walked over to the big wooden desk she insisted on buying for him because it looked 'just the part'. It had been a right royal pain getting it up the stairs and he hoped he never had to move it again. They lived in a terraced house and the third bedroom was the smallest. After their daughter had moved out Inga painted it dark green and transformed it into his 'study'. Sometimes, she was full of surprises.

Jonathan sat down in his chair and looked at the pictures on the walls. The only room that was truly his. He was surrounded by pictures of his twenty-two years in the army. There were pictures of him with every unit he served with in Northern Ireland, Iraq, Bosnia, Kosovo and Iraq a second time. Pictures of REME teams he played for. Rugby trophies and leaving presents were displayed in the bookcase beside him. He didn't know how much he would miss the army when he retired. He couldn't remember exactly why he left. He could have taken his commission and carried on but decided to call it a day. He glanced at the picture in the silver frame in front of him and his family's smiling faces.

He breathed in deeply, opened the bottom draw of his desk and pulled out a wooden box. He had carried the battered old box with him ever since basic training. In it there were more memories of his army life. A row of medals he wore once a year on Remembrance Day, an old beret with his REME badge, some spare buttons with the REME logo, letters his wife had sent to him whilst he was deployed and pendants awarded to him playing corps rugby.

He rifled through photos of friends and comrades in arms. Some had since passed on, most of them were very much alive, scattered all over the world. He was in all those pictures. In Northern Ireland working on a Land Rover, spanner in hand. In Germany, holding a 'Stein' beer mug. In Canada, on top of a tank frying some eggs on the engine. In Kenya, walking around the bush feeding monkeys. In New Zealand, sitting in a hot tub after a game of rugby. In Iraq, with a Valentine's cake sent by his wife.

There it was. He blew the dust of the surface.

He came back down the stairs and handed an old Polaroid to his wife. It was out of focus but she was able to identify her husband straight away flanked by two army nurses. It showed him in desert combats, young and fresh faced, and he was holding a tiny baby towards the camera. There was an inscription underneath the photograph.

To Corporal Montgomery, March 1ˢᵗ, Iraq 1991

30.

Inga contacted the local paper the next day and demanded to speak to someone in charge. The newspaper sent her the 'nitwit', who wrote the story of the 'body' that wasn't. Inga looked at his outstretched hand when he introduced himself.

'I'm Patrick Bucannon,' he said with a smile. 'As I already told you on the phone, Mrs Montgomery, I am very interested in running the story in tomorrow's edition.'

'Of course, you are, you little weasel,' she thought to herself but took his hand and invited him in. Toby wagged his tail and barked at the stranger. Inga led him towards the kitchen.

Under no circumstances was he going to sit in the comfy chair. Not after the things he put her through. No way.

'It was very embarrassing for me to find my name in your paper,' she said. He ignored her. 'I need to clarify some things with you, if you don't mind.' The dog expectantly looked at Patrick for his treat.

'Would you like coffee or tea, Patrick?' she replied instead. She wondered if he noticed that she was in charge here. He clearly didn't understand neither her nor the dog.

'I need some proof or any evidence you have to corroborate your story,' he continued without answering. 'We can't run a story on hearsay, you see.' She turned around and looked at him.

'Sit.' She omitted the 'please' on purpose and pointed to the only chair without padding. Patrick sat down, so did the dog.

'Tea please, Mrs Montgomery,' he said.

Inga rewarded the dog with a treat and patted him on the head. She would have liked to have patted the man's head too, but that would've been rude. She wasn't a rude person but she needed to make a point. Inga popped some filter coffee in the machine. It took her a while to froth the milk. Patrick started to look uncomfortable on the hard chair but she ignored him.

'I thought you lot had to get permission to print a person's name. Is this not some violation of the data protection act or something?' She sounded a little harsh. When she sat down on her own soft cushion, she realised she had forgotten to make his tea. How rude.

'I'm sorry, Mrs Montgomery, I wrote the article after reading the information in the police report. I should have checked with you first.'

'Call me Inga,' she said and because he looked a little frightened, she decided to forgive him. She got up, boiled the kettle and put a steaming cup of tea in front of him. 'Sugar?'

Patrick nodded, pulled out pen and paper. Inga put some biscuits in front of him.

'If you could tell me, in your own words, what happened since you found the bag?'

'The "body" in the allotment is a Republican Guard uniform.' She retrieved the box from the extension and opened the lid.

'We found this inside the uniform.' She pulled the plastic wallet out of the box, which contained the newspaper page and handed him the translation. Her finger tapped on the story about a baby being up for adoption. The journalist looked at her with expectant eyes and shrugged his shoulders.

'I don't see the connection,' he said.

With great delight, Inga told him the story of her husband, the veteran soldier, finding the baby in the desert after the First Gulf War and with a triumphant grin on her face she handed him the last piece of evidence.

'They named her Hope.'

Patrick sat back on his chair and looked from the uniform wrapped in clingfilm, to the newspaper, to the photograph. He took a sip of his tea.

'This is amazing.'

'Isn't it just.' Excited, she couldn't sit still any longer. 'Are you going to print this story?' she said and looked at him, eagerly waiting for his reply.

'I have to verify some things. Could you call your husband? I would very much like to speak to him in person. This is really extraordinary.'

Inga called Jonathan and Patrick listened as her husband told the story a second time. He rang the paper and a photographer arrived at her house ten minutes later. He took a picture of Inga holding the uniform and picked up the Polaroid picture. 'I promise to return it tomorrow,' he said.

Jonathan pulled up outside the house just as they were leaving and reluctantly agreed to pose for a photograph next to Inga, who grinned like a Cheshire cat.

'I am surprised,' Patrick said to her husband on the way out, 'that nobody ever picked up on this story.'

'Like I said to my wife. It wasn't a big deal. I'm not a hero and don't really want any fuss. If you could keep the story somewhere in the middle?' His voice sounded hopeful. 'Inga was very embarrassed last time her name appeared in your paper and we don't want to upset her again, do we? If you could make the article small, yet visible? Inga can have her five minutes of fame and I have some peace and quiet.'

The guy laughed. 'Anything for a bit of peace and quiet, hey? I see what I can do but it's up to how my editor wants to run this story. I'll do my best for you.' He winked at Jonathan and they shook hands. Jonathan waved him goodbye as he drove past him down the road.

Inga watched her husband walk up the path. She rubbed her hands together and gave her husband a hug. This was going to be huge, she could feel it.

'My hero,' she said and kissed him on the mouth. Jonathan hugged her back and said nothing.

31.

A DIFFERENT KIND OF HERO

Inga M., 54, who thought she had discovered a 'body' on her allotment,
the *Herald* reported, *discovered a very unusual item. On further
investigation the bag the police discovered on her allotment contained a
suit, which her husband identified as a former Iraqi Republican Guard
uniform. On closer examination Mr and Mrs M. found a newspaper
article relating to a baby which was discovered by a member of the
British Forces taking part in operation Desert Storm in February 1991.*

*The soldier risked his life to take the child to safety at a nearby army
field hospital. The baby girl would have died, if found only minutes later.
This soldier is Inga's husband, Jonathan M, 53. Jonathan M served in
the British Army for 22 years and was in the First Gulf War. 'Anyone
would have done the same, I'm no hero,' he said to our reporter. He
didn't know what happened to the girl after he handed her over to the
authorities.*

*He said that he found the infant in the desert near Basra, wrapped
in a blanket and a bracelet around her wrist. The nurses named the baby
'Hope'. The inscription on the inside of the bracelet read: Mohamed –
Nazreen 1986, which we presume could be the name of her parents. Our
own research shows that the baby was placed with the Red Crescent
operating in the Basra Area.*

*The appeal to the public for relatives to come forward was
successful and the little girl was taken home by an aunt and uncle. The
names on the papers received from the British Red Cross are Mr Omar
and Mrs Safiya Abdullah. The girl would be 27 now.*

*Many official documents were destroyed during the Second Gulf
War and we don't know what happened to the little girl afterwards.
However, the official papers from 1991 suggest that her adoptive parents
came from the Baghdad area and were visiting relatives in Basra at the*

time. We feel that it is our duty to re-unite this little girl with the man who saved her life.

If you have any information, especially the Iraqi community with relatives in Basrad, please contact the press office. There is also a website and an appeal on Facebook and Twitter. Dear readers, let's make this happen. Let's use the power of social media to re-unite this reluctant hero with the little girl he saved from certain death.

Jonathan thought that Patrick had overstretched his creative licence a lot and studied the pictures at the side of the article. He sighed, folded the paper together and looked out of the window. So much for 'Brothers in Arms' on civvy street.

32.

A man, identifying himself as a reporter from the *Herald*, had turned up on his doorstep. His name was Patrick and he asked him if he had leased a plot of land on Whinbury Street in the late nineties.

Hakim was surprised that they had found him so fast. Records. Everything was stored on a computer these days. He didn't deny that he leased the plot but said that he didn't know anything about a buried Republican Guard uniform. The shed was already there. He was a Kurd and an enemy of the Saddam regime. He told the journalist that he would speak to him again tomorrow, when he had more time.

'The story will be in the paper tonight, sir. But I can come back in a day or two and have a chat with you and your wife. Maybe she recollects anything unusual?'

Hakim read the article again. The uniform by itself, the forgotten newspaper stuffed into the breast pocket, he could have explained to the reporter but not Nazreen. After all these years, his time was up.

He would lose her. She would never look at him again, never speak to him again, he might as well be dead. If the authorities found out his real identity he would be deported and he would stand trial. He wasn't frightened of being punished but he couldn't bear the thought of being separated from Nazreen who was innocent in all of this.

He should have told her the night he found out but he forgot after everything that happened and afterwards he didn't find the courage. He was frightened that Nazreen would not believe that he didn't know the child was alive. She would accuse him of leaving her baby in the desert to die. Did he know she was still breathing when he put her on the floor and surrounded her with stones? He couldn't remember. All he did remember was that Nazreen was going to die if he hadn't carried on with their journey. Even to him, it sounded hollow. It sounded like he wanted her and not the baby. She would never forgive him.

33.

They dragged the men from the hut and undressed their bodies. They covered the blood with sand till the patches seemed to be invisible to the naked eye. They burnt the men's clothes and put their bodies into the boat, which he untied and pushed into the stream. Their boat disappeared into the distance being carried down the Euphrates by the current.

Hopefully, the bodies weren't going to be discovered for a while. At least nobody would be able to identify them by their faces.

They continued their journey on horseback. Nazreen had never been on the back of a horse, but she soon learned how to keep her balance and they left the hut and the dead men far behind. He prayed that the old man would keep quiet about the man in uniform, visiting him on the night of the men's disappearance. He couldn't rely on his silence but he was confident that they had enough time to get further north, where they could hide in the mountains.

The first day they didn't camp. They avoided Karbala altogether and took the road alongside the lake. When the horses were tired they let them graze for an hour and continued to travel on foot.

They stopped in one of the tiny villages along the lake and while Hakim bought a mule, provisions and food for the horses, Nazreen bought a pair of trousers on the market. She showed them to him before they left.

'Look, Hakim,' she said, holding her dress up by the hem. 'So much better for riding, don't you think?'

They rode all day and when the sun began to set, found some boulders at the side of the lake. He tied up the horses and lit a fire.

She sat at the edge of the lake, cooling her feet in the water. Nazreen thought about the mountains they would have to cross. Were they still covered in snow? She wondered if the snow was permanent. She would love to go right up to the top and feel the snow in her hands. It had been so hot today. Unbearable. She stood up and waded into the water. It was not cold but after the heat of the day it was cool enough to give relief.

'What were you thinking about?' Hakim asked, handing her a cup of tea. She touched his hand and pulled him down to her side.

'I feel so small under all these stars. It feels like we are just a speck of dust in Allah's universe.

'Look at the sky. Isn't it beautiful? I feel like I never appreciated life until now. I always felt that I was someone's property. First my father's, then my husband's. I didn't see the beauty of the stars above. I didn't want to live and if it wouldn't have been for the baby I wouldn't be here,' she whispered. 'Now, thanks to you, I feel free. I'm free to make my own decisions. I look at the stars and I'm glad to be alive.

'Thank you, Hakim,' she said and leaned her head against his shoulder. He tried to breathe normally but was very much aware of the warmth of her body next to him. He put an arm around her shoulder and moved closer. He took the cup and put it on the floor, lifted her chin so he could see her face. The fire was reflecting in her eyes. She looked so beautiful and her half-open mouth full and inviting. He moved closer and gently placed his lips on hers. Nazreen didn't recoil. She enjoyed the taste of his lips on her mouth and the heat of his body. She turned towards him and her hand travelled up his spine. He felt her fingers at the base of his neck. Her fingers clutched the top of his shirt, pulling his body closer into hers, kissing him harder. She fell backwards and pulled him with her so he laid half on top of her. His hands were entangled in her hair. Suddenly as if woken from a dream, he gently tried to free himself out of their embrace.

'No, *Habibi,* we shouldn't...' he said out of breath. She looked at him rejected and hurt.

'I know,' she said quietly. 'I'm spoilt and without honour. It was foolish of me to think you could go on and love me again like you did when we were children!' Tears were beginning to pool at the corner of her eyes.

'Don't cry, my love. It's nothing like you think.' He propped himself up on one arm. 'I've waited for this moment for so long. You have no idea how hard this is for me. I have loved you for such a long time. I must do right by you. Don't you see? I've let you down so many times in the past and I promised myself to marry you before you know... I need to get it right. Nazreen.

'Come here, let me just hold you close to me for now.' She sighed deeply but laid still beside him.

He enjoyed feeling the weight of her head in the arch of his shoulder; hugging each other they fell asleep. An owl hooted into the night. He thought that he'd never been happier.

34.

They had left Lake Quadisiyah and the town of Haditha far behind and made their way towards the Syrian border. They had to climb through rough terrain, leading the horses by their reins. Hakim was leading the way and talking about what their lives would be like once they left Iraq behind.

'When we are safe, I will marry you and we will live in a house with a garden. I will go out to work and you will look after our children. We will have at least four,' he said. 'Two boys and two girls. You will be a wonderful mother to them. You will have the most beautiful clothes, I promise I will make you happy. You will never have to worry about anything again, as long as I'm with you,' he said to her, talking over his shoulder.

She loved it when he talked about their lives together. He made it sound so easy. She felt a stitch in her heart when he talked about their children, thinking about the one she had lost and her hand reached into her pocket where she kept the little lock of hair. 'I will never forget you as long as I live,' she said, clutching the lock in her hand but yes, she would be a good mother to his children and the best wife she could be.

They climbed higher into the mountains and although the sun was hot during the day, the nights became colder the higher they climbed on the ancient trail left by the shepherds. One day they came across an old man, his donkey struggling with a heavy load. She handed Hakim her bracelets, the only things she still possessed of value, to trade for one of his sheep. Hakim refused to take them and traded the Kalashnikov instead.

It was getting dark and they invited the man to join them. They didn't have much else left to share but Hakim slaughtered the sheep and Nazreen cooked a stew on the open fire.

'Where have you come from?' he asked the shepherd.

'I have been in Syria and sold some of these sheep. Now I'm going back. Next month I will go again. This is my life,' the old man replied.

'Why are you going back to a country that does not treat its people well?' Hakim asked, sitting together, puffing out smoke into the cold mountain air from the old man's pipe.

'Where else would I go?' the old man replied. 'I am going back to my family, my wife and children. What would they do without me? Saddam's power doesn't reach this far and we live our lives as we have done for hundreds of years. I love Iraq, but don't have to love the man ruling Iraq. We are far away from Baghdad and I am just an unimportant trader of goods. He has no interest in me. Anyway, what would be the point in trading one Saddam Hussein for one Hafez al-Assad? Are they not all the same?

'Why are you leaving?' he asked curiously. Hakim thought about what to tell the old man and whether he could be trusted.

'I have been in two wars and hoped for a new beginning after the people's revolution but Saddam is still in power. Now, Nazreen and I have decided to go away and I must make a new start somewhere else.' He looked at Nazreen.

'She is Shia, I am Sunni. It didn't matter before but I don't think anybody would allow us to be together, especially not now. I love her and only Allah should judge whether I am worthy of her.'

The man nodded. 'Wise words from a man as young as you are,' he said.

On hearing those words, she looked up and smiled at Hakim.

'I can't wait to be a mother,' she said quietly and he saw the pain in her eyes. In the morning they said their goodbyes and walked away in opposite directions. The old man, back to his wife and children, Hakim and Nazreen towards a new life.

They had passed the summit and were on the descent. Looking out onto the vast landscape below, the river, that snaked its way through the mountain, dotted with green bushes and feed for the horses, he felt hopeful. Soon they would be safe.

He had got everything he ever wanted and soon she would be his in the eyes of Allah.

They reached the bottom of the plateau on the afternoon of a lovely September day. The wind was blowing in their faces and her hair was flowing in the wind like a black veil. She was galloping in front of him, laughing with joy. He couldn't take his eyes off her. She seemed so happy and carefree. When he caught up with her he grabbed hold of her reins. Hakim dismounted and caught her by the waist, helping her off the back of the horse. Her cheeks were rosy from the ride and her eyes were sparkling with life. She was breathless and never looked more beautiful than in that moment.

He lifted her high into the air and whirled her around, which made her laugh out loud. Sliding her body through his hands slowly, her face came into focus and he couldn't help but kiss her full lips that were still smiling at the sides. She wrapped her arms around the back of his neck and pulled herself closer into him, returning his kiss passionately. He kissed her back till he thought he would run out of air.

'Nazreen, you need to stop.' He placed her feet down on the floor. 'Please, you need to stop.' Nazreen looked at him.

She thought she had known love before but that was a different kind of love. It was the love for a mother, the love for a friend and the love for a child. She didn't know what love between a man and a woman really felt like; her marriage had been a transaction between two families. This new feeling of warmth in her heart and the passion he ignited in her body felt like love. Having him near her, protect her, kiss her, felt like love. She didn't want it to end. She didn't care whether they were married in front of Allah. Allah was everywhere, wasn't he? She pulled his face back down to hers and continued the kiss he cut short.

'I don't care,' she whispered in his ear, moving her body closer to his. 'Come to me. I love you.'

She had fallen asleep in his embrace. He felt guilty but could not deny his contentment. She had spoken the words he longed to hear all his life and felt he couldn't be happier. He looked at the stars above and thanked Allah for this woman.

With her by his side he could be a better man. He would be able to forget his past and the monster he had become. She healed the wound in his heart and made everything new. He would never disappoint her and she would be proud of the man he was going to become. She would never discover the man he had been, the monster who killed and tortured and had left her baby in the desert for dead.

The old shepherd had been right. Why leave one dictator behind to live under the regime of another? He decided to go further away, to a country they didn't know, where they had to start over, without being haunted by memories. He closed his eyes and snuggled closer into her body, knowing he would never let her go.

35.

The next day they reached the banks of the Euphrates and rode along the river till they arrived at Dayr az Zawr. Hakim sold the horses and the mule and they boarded a train to Damascus. She looked happy, gazing out of the window, holding his hand underneath a blanket. The landscape started to change. Soon they saw Aspen and poplars growing by the side of the tracks, apricot and nut orchards, olive groves and vegetable gardens as the train flew by. They would soon arrive at the main train station.

Hakim's uniform was still in the bottom of his bag, along with the gun, the jewellery and gold he had stolen from Kuwait. He would deal with all of that once they had found a hotel. He needed passports and a new identity and then he would marry her. They would be man and wife before leaving Damascus to start their new life.

They rented a room in the first hotel they passed close to the train station. It wasn't glamorous but it was clean.

'I have to go out, Nazreen, to run a couple of errands,' he said taking her hands. 'You are safe here. I will be some time. Please, don't leave the room till I'm back. I will be as quick as I can.

'I know I promised not to leave you ever again but where I'm going you won't be welcome and you will be safer here. You can order some food from the reception and when I come back we will go out for something to eat. OK?'

She nodded. 'Be quick, Hakim. I understand.' He kissed her quickly and she locked the door after he left. It felt strange after the long month in the desert. Being enclosed in a room by walls, having running water and a bed felt strange. She opened the window and listened to the traffic outside. It was odd listening to the hustle and bustle of civilisation after so many months of silence. Nazreen went to the bathroom and ran herself a bath. She discarded her dusty clothes in a heap on the floor. Surrounded by bubbles she felt glorious and clean. She couldn't bear to put the clothes back on after her bath and sat in the chair by the window wrapped in a towel. She was hungry but couldn't find the courage to order anything off the menu. How could she put her dirty clothes back on and open the door to room service? She laid on the bed looking at the fan on the ceiling. Round and round.

She must have nodded off because it was dark outside when she woke from a knock on the door. Draping the bed sheet around her she walked to the door.

'Who is it?' she asked.

'It's me, *Habibi*, open the door.'

She unlocked the door, opened it in a hurry, dropping the sheet in the process. For a moment he just looked at her and drank in the beautiful curves of her body, her long flowing hair covering her breasts, her eyes still blurry from sleep and her big smile. Hakim stepped into the room and dropped the parcels on the bed. He pulled her in his arms.

'I missed you,' he said and smelled the shampoo in her hair. 'You smell like the peaches I bought,' he said.

'And you smell like... well I better not say it.' She pulled away from him, scrunched her nose and pointed to the bathroom.

'You need to take a shower,' she said. He picked the sheet off the floor.

'And you need to wrap this back around you before I change my mind, smelly or not.' He slapped her on her bum. 'Go and have a look in those parcels while I have a shower.'

He heard paper being ripped and her excited cries when he stepped into the shower and he smiled. When he opened the door to the room he found her, surrounded by her new clothes, fast asleep on the bed, still holding a half-eaten peach. He tidied the clothes away and ate the rest of the peach, sitting on the chair next to the window. He'd managed to open a bank account and had deposited everything he had into the account. Tomorrow he was going to take her to the Iraqi Embassy in Damascus and report their passports as stolen. It was going to be risky but he doubted that anybody would check their story if he used her husband's name. Not so soon after the war. But that was tomorrow. Tonight, he would let her sleep peacefully and hold her body close to him.

In the morning she dressed in her new underwear and paraded round the room in the skirt and blouse he bought. She tried on the new shoes and struggled with the heels, nearly falling over.

'I will break my legs walking in these. Could you not have bought some sandals?' She walked unsteadily trying to balance her body and laughed.

'You will have to look your best today, Nazreen. We are going to the embassy and report our passports as stolen.'

'We are what?' She turned around in surprise and sat on the chair. He explained what they were about to do and she looked at him skeptically. 'And you think this is really going to work?'

'I'm ninety-nine percent sure it will. If we can keep our cool and stick to the same story. Do you think you can do that for me?'

'What about that one percent, Hakim?'

He shrugged his shoulders and put his jacket on. '*Inshallah*,' he said. '*Inshallah.*'

They had breakfast together and it felt strange. The people around her looked so normal, chatting about the day ahead, eating their breakfasts, laughing. For a fleeting moment she wished she was back in the desert, just with him and the stars for company. She straightened her spine and took a deep breath. 'Let's do this,' she said to Hakim, put the scarf around her head and stood up.

Afterwards she felt like skipping through the gates of the embassy but she contained herself at the last minute. It had been strangely straightforward. The passports were going to be ready at the end of the week and the embassy was even going to pay for their train tickets back to Iraq. She was ecstatic with joy and grabbed Hakim's hand.

'What do you want to do now, Nazreen? Do you want to get married?' he asked her, licking the ice cream dripping off his cone. They sat on a bench in a park near the embassy, pigeons were cooing round their feet, eating the crumbs that she dropped on the floor.

'I do,' she said with conviction. 'Do we have to get married though since on paper you are already my husband?' She gave him a cheeky smile.

'All right,' he said. 'We don't then!' He shrugged his shoulders and pretended to be all right with the idea.

'Oh no,' she said. 'You promised!'

He turned to her and laughed. 'Of course, we are going to be blessed. Let's get you back to the hotel and I will arrange everything.'

Nazreen settled back in a chair with a pot of steaming hot tea in front of her in the lobby. She had been bored alone in the room, waiting for his return. She felt content, watching the cars and people go by. A moped pulled up at the entrance and a man entered the hotel with a big white box. She overheard her name and walked over to the girl at the reception.

'This is for you,' the receptionist said to her holding the box.

'You are one lucky lady,' she said to Nazreen, looking at the name on the box. 'This is from one of the best bridal shops in town. Congratulations.' She handed her the box. 'If you need anything else please let me know.'

Nazreen climbed the stairs to the room in a trance and put the box carefully on the bed. There was a note attached to the string. *Do not open till tomorrow* it said.

She couldn't resist and lifted the lid. The dress was stunning. She saw dark green velvet, decorated with golden peacocks, their tails floating behind them. She pulled the dress from the box and walked over to the window. The middle part, running from the top to the bottom was made from gold satin, studded with little gemstones that sparkled in the afternoon sunshine. The sleeves were delicate chiffon. It had a matching headscarf and shoes decorated with gems in all colours. There was also a smaller box which contained a pair of ruby earrings. Nazreen was overwhelmed by Hakim's generosity and sat in silence, staring at the dress in her hands.

Was she really going to wear this dress tomorrow? It didn't feel real. She didn't deserve all this attention. Was she worth all this? She folded the dress and put it carefully back in the box, closed the lid and tied the string back around the sides. How could she ever repay him? She sat on the chair in front of the open window, looking at the box in front of her when he knocked on the door.

'*Habibi*,' he greeted her, bringing more parcels. 'I see they delivered the dress. Good. Did you have a peek? I bet you did!'

'I never,' she said looking at him innocently. He had seen too many interrogations to know that she was lying but it didn't matter. She was beaming from ear to ear and that made him happy.

'Come on, let's go out for something to eat. I'm starving.'

The rest of the afternoon they spent just like any tourist visiting Damascus. It was a beautiful city. They walked through the old town, immersed in the smell of the spices. Little shops, one next to the other, sold food and sweets, clothes and household goods, souvenirs and Persian rugs. It was an assault on her senses. They visited Salahedin's Mausoleum, the Al Azem Palace and the Umayyad Mosque. By the time they arrived back at the hotel, her feet were sore and he carried her up the stairs to the room. She fell asleep almost immediately, dreaming of the dress she was going to wear in the morning.

When she woke up she found a note on his pillow, a faint smell of aftershave was still lingering in the room. *Open the box and come downstairs once you're ready* it said. She took a bath, dried her hair and put on the dress. It fitted perfectly. She looked at the person in the mirror. Was that really her? She looked like a princess and the earrings were sparkling almost as bright as her eyes. She took the scarf, draped it around her shoulders and was thankful he'd chosen pumps instead of high heels.

She saw him waiting at the bottom of the stairs. He wore a black velvet suit with a white shirt. The waistcoat underneath showed a golden peacock and hen looking at each other. His beard had been trimmed and his hair was cut neatly at the back but his fringe was still the same. He looked dashing and she nervously made her way down the stairs, one foot at the time.

Hakim looked up at her descending the stairs and thought she would never look more beautiful to him than on that day. It took his breath away. She stood on the last step and looked at him nervously.

'Can I go like this, Hakim?' she said.

He was silent, stepped in front of her and kissed her, forgetting all about the other people in the lobby.

'I have never seen anything or anyone more beautiful than you, Nazreen. I am the proudest man alive. Come on, let's not let them wait.'

He took her by the hand and led her past the people in the lobby to a waiting taxi.

They were blessed by the imam and, when he held her hand and slipped the ring on her finger, she looked up with a smile. She saw a tear, slowly running down his cheek. She wiped it away with her fingers.

'No more tears, Hakim,' she said. 'No more. I'm yours now, forever.'

'There is one more trip to make before we leave this life behind,' he said when they were back in the taxi. He told the driver their next destination. The car stopped in front of Sayyidah Ruqayya Mosque. The mosque was built around the martyred remains of a four-year-old little girl name Ruqayya bint Husaym, also known as Sukayna, the young daughter of Husayn ibn Ali, a grandson of the prophet, who was killed in the battle of Karbala. They stepped out of the car and he led her under the shaded arches at the side of the building.

'Have you got the lock of hair with you, Nazreen?' He didn't really have to ask. She pulled the cloth from her pocket and showed it to him. Hakim pulled a little box from his pocket. 'I bought this for you. I thought it would be nice if you kept the lock of her hair in it. I brought you here so you might say goodbye to her properly. Maybe it will help you to reconcile if you pray at Sukayna's grave.' He took the hair and placed it in the locket. 'I will wait for you here.'

She took off her shoes, entered the gate and covered her head with the black headscarf a woman handed her. She walked through the courtyard, past the impressive prayer room and entered the room with Sukayna's shrine. It was beautiful and the closer she walked towards the gold and silver cage-like structure, the more peaceful she felt. The doors, made of pure gold with mirror works on the roof and walls, illuminated by the reflection of the golden dome directly above, invited her to step closer. She leaned her head against the stone structure, clutching the locket in her fist against the cold marble of the tomb. Silent tears fell from her eyes as she started to pray.

'Sukayna, hear me and my prayer. Look after my child for me, great granddaughter of the Prophet Muhammad, peace be upon him. I loved my child even though I never met her. She was part of me as I was part of her. I will never forget her. Rest in peace, my angel, till we see each other again to find your grandmother in paradise on judgement day and bless Hakim, without him I wouldn't be here today,' she ended and put the locket around her neck. When she stepped back outside into the evening sunshine, she felt peaceful. The visit had cleansed her soul and she felt reborn. Hakim was waiting for her where he left as promised and embraced her quietly.

'Thank you, Hakim. Thank you for everything. Thank you for today and all this.' She touched the locket she felt on her heart and looked up at him. 'The past is in the past. From now on there will be just you, me and our future together. I love you so much, I sometimes find it hard to breathe.

'We can go now,' she said, leaning her head against his chest. She could feel his steady heartbeat and knew she was safe in his arms. He took her hand and placed a gentle kiss on the ring on her finger.

'I love you too. More than I'll ever be able to say because there are no words.'

Hand in hand they walked over to a waiting taxi and it took them to the banks of the river Barada, where it stopped in front of a hotel. He stepped around the car, opened her door and took her hand. 'Tonight, you shall be treated like a princess,' he said with a smile and led her up the marble steps. On entering through the big double doors, she felt like royalty. Nazreen looked at Hakim.

'We can't possibly afford this,' she whispered and he smiled back at her.

'Only the best for you on your wedding day, *Habibi*. I would give you the stars in the sky if I could.'

He talked to the man at the reception desk while she stood and tried to take it all in. It was like she had stepped into the pages of *Arabian Nights*.

In the centre of the hall was a fountain covered in the most beautiful mosaic pattern of blue and gold. Water sprang from the mouths of tiny dragons into the pool at the bottom. The trellis on the walls were covered in hibiscus flowers and jasmine and big baskets of ferns and patterned lanterns were suspended from the ceiling. An enormous crystal chandelier sparkled in the middle of the dome above the fountain. There were huge Arabian windows on one side of the wall decorated in arabesque patterns of blue, green and yellow. Under the archways in front of her people sat in plush seating areas overflowing with cushions. She could see the cloud and smell the sweet perfume of the flowers. The tiled stone floor was covered with luxurious Persian carpets, little wooden tables were surrounded by dark red leather chairs. To her it looked like a palace.

'Come on, my princess,' said a voice behind her. 'I have arranged for the best room in the house.' They took the elevator to the top of the building and he opened the door.

'Hakim,' she said looking up at him. 'I'm not worth all of this. It's like I'm having a dream.'

'*Habibi*, you're worth more than life itself.' He picked her up, carried her into the room and put her down by the end of the most enormous bed she had ever seen. He opened the door to the balcony to let in the cool evening air. She ran past him and looked out over the city.

'Come and have a look at the lights, Hakim,' she said excitedly. 'It's beautiful, don't you think?'

Standing behind her, he brushed her hair over one shoulder and leaned forward.

'You're beautiful, Nazreen. More beautiful than the lights of the city and the stars in the sky,' he whispered in her ear. Hakim kissed her gently on the nape of her neck which made her shiver. He slowly unfastened the zip of her dress and more kisses exposed the flesh on her shoulders till the dress fell to the floor with a gently swoosh. He continued kissing her shoulder and she could feel the gentle touch of his hands caressing her back. He unfastened her bra, exposing her breasts to the cool night air. He cupped her breasts with both hands from behind and gently squeezed. A moan escaped from her lips. He turned her around and their eyes met for a second. He pulled her closer. She closed her eyes when his lips touched hers. Very gently, his tongue explored every inch of her mouth till she felt her legs give way from under her. He picked her up, carried her inside the room and placed her gently on the bed.

He stood beside the bed looking down on her. He took off his clothes, his eyes never leaving hers. He looked so handsome and strong.

'This is what love feels like. This is the feeling my mother told me about,' she thought to herself and she held out her hand, inviting him into her arms.

They didn't leave the room the next day. They slept and made love, ordered room service when they were hungry. They were drunk on happiness. At first, she was sad when they had to leave and return to their hotel by the train station but it didn't matter where they stayed, they were together. At the end of the week they picked up their passports and the train tickets from the embassy. He went to a travel agent and purchased plane tickets to London.

36.

When they arrived in the United Kingdom, they walked over to the nearest border control officer and instead of showing their passports Hakim told the officer that they wanted asylum.

'Are you prepared to lie, Nazreen?' he'd said on the plane. 'They will separate us and I won't be with you for a while. Do you think you can manage without me? I am depending entirely on you from now on. If we are going to be allowed to stay depends on the story you are telling the authorities, *Habibi*.'

'Tell me what I must say,' she said and took his hand. 'I can do it if you're telling me what I must say.'

'You need to stay as close to real events as you can, my love, but your scars haven't been inflicted upon you by Mohamed any more. That's the only thing you must remember. Your father was picked up by the Mukhabarat and they shot your mother in the street. You're sure that he's been killed because he never came home and you buried your mother in the garden. You hid in the house and then they came back for you. They interrogated you. Show them your scars. Can you do that for me?'

'I'll try,' she said and looked at the floor. 'It won't be easy but I'll do my best, Hakim. What are you going to say? They won't let you stay. You haven't got any scars to show them and they will send you back.' Her voice trembled and he could hear the panic in it.

'They won't send me back, *Habibi*. I'm your husband. Tell them that you were released and that you came to our house in Basra. Tell them the Mukhabarat said they were coming for me next and that we packed our bags just as the war broke out. Tell them about our journey through the desert, about the time the Mukhabarat nearly raped you. Tell them that if we hadn't left Iraq, they would have found us and killed us. You need to convince the person in front of you that we will be sentenced to death if we're going to be returned to Iraq. Do you think you can, Nazreen?'

'But will they understand me?' she asked. 'I don't speak English yet, Hakim. What if they don't understand me and send us back straight away?'

He smiled at her and squeezed her hand. She was so sweet in her naivety.

'England is a civilised country, *Habibi*. They'll have an interpreter who will translate for you.'

'But what if he translates it all wrong and I have to sign a confession?'

He burst out into laughter and took her hand. 'I love you so much. They won't beat a confession out of you, trust me. I will back you up all the way only from another room. Can you remember the date the soldiers picked your father up? They might be able to find some paperwork, although I doubt it.'

Reassured by his presence, she put one arm through his. 'I will do as you say. You're Mohamed, but Mohamed in name only and the scars on my body are his and not yours.'

'That's the new Nazreen. I'm proud of you. Let's get a few hours' sleep. Soon we will be truly free.'

As predicted, the border control officer sat them down in two separate rooms. They were given a cup of tea and waited for an interpreter to arrive. When the door opened Nazreen jumped off her chair in fright and spilled her tea all over the table.

'I'm so sorry, sir,' she said repeatedly, trying to wipe the liquid with her sleeve. The interpreter interrupted her and sat her gently back on the chair.

'Please sit, madam, there's no need to panic here. We will clean this up in no time. Can you let me have a look at your passport in the meantime and we take it from there?'

'Karen,' he shouted down the corridor. 'We have a spillage in interview room 3. Can you bring me a cloth, please? Can I also have a cup of coffee? It might take some time.'

It took three long hours before they were back together. The border control officer listened to the interpreter and before they could stop her, Nazreen had stood up and dropped her dress to the floor. Both men quickly stood up which made their chairs fall over. Speechless they looked upon her and the scars on her body. They turned around and the interpreter told her to put her clothes back on. Nazreen sat back on her chair, bowing her head in shame, looking at her hands in her lap. The border patrol officer turned around and poured a cup of water from a jug and put the cup in front of her. Nazreen picked it up with shaking hands and took a sip.

'I think we're done here,' he said and picked up the paperwork and her passport. 'If you want to stay here, madam, I will talk to my colleague and I'll be right back.' She looked at the interpreter.

'What's going to happen to me?' she asked. 'Is he going to arrest me? Is he sending us back to Iraq?'

'I don't know. Let's wait and see. Do you want anything? More water perhaps?'

Nazreen shook her head. After what seemed like an eternity to her the officer opened the door and sat back at his desk in front of her.

'Mrs Ahmed, I have spoken with my colleague and I'm happy to say we have decided that your request to apply for asylum has been granted. We will re-unite you with your husband. A case worker is on the way and will explain what will happen next. If you would follow me, please.'

She burst out into tears and the interpreter handed her a box of tissues.

'Now, now,' he said. 'I hope those are happy tears. Come on now. It's not over yet but you have made the first step.' He followed her outside and they walked along the corridor to another interview room. The officer knocked on the door.

'Enter,' a voice said from behind and when the man opened the door, she saw Hakim who stood up from his chair. She hurried past the interpreter and fell into his arms, sobbing her heart out.

'Nazreen, *Habibi*, everything is going to be all right. We're safe now. Come and sit with me.' They pulled up a chair and she sat down, looking at the floor.

'Mr and Mrs Ahmed. A case worker will be with you shortly. In the meantime, we need to take your fingerprints and your pictures. Mrs Ahmed, if you could go with this lady, she will take pictures of your injuries. We're keeping your passports for now but you will be given a photocopy of it. Your case worker will explain what happens next.

'Welcome to the United Kingdom,' he said and left.

37.

They sat in a waiting room after they'd been processed. Their bag had been collected and checked but Hakim knew they wouldn't find anything but their clothes. Nazreen had followed a woman to a different room and she had taken photographs of every scar and burn mark on her body. There was a knock on the door and they both turned their heads. A woman appeared in the doorway. Her blonde hair was pushed back in a ponytail and she was wearing a grey suit and blue blouse. The glasses she wore made her look older than she probably was. She carried a folder under her arm which she laid down on the table. Hakim felt uneasy having a woman in charge of their future but he was willing to listen what she had to say. The woman gestured for the interpreter to translate and looked at the couple in front of her.

'Hello,' she said. 'How are you? My name is Susan and I am your case worker. Your request to apply for asylum has now been registered and you are now in our system. Do you know what that means?' She looked at them both and waited for the translator to catch up.

'We can stay here?' Hakim asked hopefully. She nodded.

'It means that you're under the temporary protection of the United Kingdom. Nobody will harm you or your wife while you are here. If you qualify you will be granted permission to remain in the UK as a refugee. This is known as the right to remain. After five years you can apply to settle in the UK but we're getting ahead of ourselves. For now, we will take you to a hostel. There you will remain and report to me once a week. I will give you my details. You will be interviewed again by a separate case worker. They will notify you by letter. You MUST attend this interview and you MUST report to me once a week. I can't state strongly enough how important this is for your application. Do you understand?' She looked at them sternly over the rim of her glasses and nodded at the interpreter.

They both nodded in acknowledgement. 'We understand,' they said in unison.

'It can take up to six months for your application to be processed, sometimes it takes longer. It depends on each individual case. You're not allowed to work till this case has been resolved but you can use the NHS for medical emergencies and you can claim support for your personal needs like soap and food, which come in the form of vouchers. I will give you the necessary forms to fill in, which are going to be in your own language. Do you understand?'

They looked at the interpreter and nodded.

'Have you got any questions for me?' She looked at them and smiled.

Hakim swallowed his pride and smiled back at her and took Nazreen's hand. 'We don't have any questions but we want to thank you very much, don't we Nazreen?' Nazreen nodded her head and looked at Susan.

'We are very grateful to you. I don't know how we can ever repay you.'

'Don't thank me yet, love,' Susan replied. 'Nothing has been decided yet. If you want to follow me. We will take you to your accommodation so you can rest. Please take all your belongings. I will be back with you in a minute with the photocopy of your passports which are going to be kept safe and the forms I talked about in a minute.'

They followed Susan and the interpreter to her car. Nazreen looked out of the window and stared in awe at the hustle and bustle in the streets. Men and women hurrying past the shop windows, dressed in winter jackets, hats and scarfs. A big red bus blocked the road in front of them and she could hear the impatient beeping of the people in the cars behind them, trying to get home in time for supper. It was getting dark and the street lights illuminated the outside of a big brick building. 'Hounslow Hostel' it said above the door. She got out and looked fearfully at the plane above making its descent into Heathrow Airport. It was very loud and panicked she threw herself on the floor, covering her head with her arms, waiting for the impact of the bomb. The interpreter looked at her shivering body at his feet and picked her up off the floor with Hakim.

'That's Concorde,' he said. 'You will see it twice a day. Isn't it a beauty?'

They stopped at an office next to the entrance and Susan talked to the person behind the desk. She handed him a wallet which he locked in a filing cabinet behind him. He took a pair of keys off a shelf and handed it to Susan.

'This is your room key,' she said. 'You will be staying in room number 134. There is a kettle in the room and a fridge. A starter kit of tea and coffee is provided. Unfortunately, there are no bathrooms in the rooms but there is a shared shower block and a separate toilet at the end of each corridor. You will find a pair of towels in your room which are your responsibility. You will report to the front desk every day in the morning and at night. When you leave the premises, you will let the clerk know and hand in the key. This will be given back to you on your return. There is a communal area with a kitchen at the end of this hall where you'll be able to cook. I have a food voucher for you, which you must sign for. This is a list of shops they can be used in and this is a map of the area. I will be in the office on the other side of the room every Thursday when you need to report to me. I know this is a lot to take in but you will find a guide in your language in your room. Any questions?'

Nazreen looked at her husband with tired eyes. She didn't. She was exhausted and wanted to go to sleep. The translator handed Hakim his card and pointed to the telephone in the lobby.

'If you need me or you have a problem, mate, don't hesitate to call. There is also a telephone number of a help organisation on the back. OK?'

'Thank you very much again, friend.' Hakim shook his hand and nodded at Susan. 'Thank you. You're very kind.' He watched as they left together.

'Just you and me now, Nazreen. Let's find the room we're staying in. Come on, don't go to sleep just yet.' They followed the signs to the first floor. They could hear music being played behind some of the doors they passed. Sometimes they heard voices talking in a different language. They passed a man in the corridor just wearing a towel and Nazreen hid behind Hakim who looked angry. Number 134. He opened the door and pushed Nazreen through the entrance.

'I don't think I'm going to like *him* very much,' he said.

'I hardly noticed,' Nazreen replied and fell onto the bed. She was asleep within minutes.

38.

At first, they kept to their room. Hakim accompanied her to the washroom and the toilet till she remarked that he was worse than Mohamed.

'Hakim,' she complained one day. 'We have been here now for two weeks and I'm not doing anything on my own. I haven't even been to the kitchen yet. The only time you let me out of this room is when I need the toilet or we meet with Susan downstairs. I can't be in here any longer. It's like a prison. I need to get out of here!'

'I know, I know,' he replied. 'I just don't want you to get hurt.'

'There's nothing for me to do here in this room. I'm going crazy. One of these days I'm going to throw myself out of this window. See…' She tried to open the window but it wouldn't budge.

He smiled at her. 'They have nailed them shut on the outside, darling, so people don't jump out of them!'

'I need to see other people, speak with other women. I feel so isolated. Please take me shopping with you at least. It's not fair. You can go wherever you please but you make me remain in this room like a prisoner. I might as well have stayed in Iraq.' She sat back down on the bed with a huff.

'I'm sorry, Nazreen. I thought you would feel safer up here. If you want, I will show you the shop I buy our food. There's a park nearby. Do you want to go and feed the ducks?'

She clapped her hands together and put on her shoes.

'Hold your horses, it's still freezing out there. They have a "thrift" shop downstairs in the hall. Maybe we'll find a jacket and hat for you.'

It was hard to keep up with her running down the corridor, talking excitedly. She found a jacket which was a little too small and a hat that was a little too big. She looked at herself in the mirror and laughed when she put the hat over her head scarf.

'Oh dear, Hakim, just have a look at me! Hello, I'm from a foreign country and I can't dress.' She laughed at her reflection. 'At least you're going to be warm. Come on. Let's go.'

She enjoyed everything about that day. She wasn't bothered that people stared at her. It began to snow and she tried to catch snowflakes with her tongue. She enjoyed pushing the trolley around the shop, studying the different packets on the shelves. She was like a child in a sweet shop. In the end she purchased a bar of soap. It smelled heavenly. They walked hand in hand through the park and fed the ducks on the pond. They bought some rice, lemons and anise and when they returned, he accompanied her to the kitchen where she cooked rice and lemons and made flatbreads together. She met a woman from Iraq who she invited to share their meal and after a short while they began to talk as if they'd been friends forever.

She had to promise him to never go anywhere unaccompanied and he let her go and talk to the other women in the kitchen without him.

Days turned into weeks and weeks into months. They had attended their second interview and Susan made them feel hopeful. Nazreen nearly gave herself away one day in calling him Hakim. Susan looked at her puzzled.

'My brother was called Hakim so sometimes I call my husband Hakim. It's like when you're confused, you see.'

'You've got to be more careful Nazreen,' he scolded her later. 'I hope Susan isn't going to make a big deal out of this.'

They both started to attend English classes once a week in the communal hall. Nazreen loved the homework. They took trips to the library and started to read children's books. It was a lot of fun laying on the bed, reading to each other. He laughed at the strange sound of her voice when she talked in English. They rang the help organisation on the back of the card from the interpreter and joined their meetings and evening prayers. Afterwards, she would sit with the other women in a circle on the floor exchanging stories from home. Nazreen never faltered and he was getting used to being called Mohamed in public.

One day in early July 1992 Susan sent a message that she would like to see them in her office on a Monday instead of the usual Thursday. She was waiting for them, the interpreter already sat on a chair at the side of her desk.

'Come in and sit down you two. I have news. This is it. Are you ready?'

Nazreen took Hakim's hand and they sat in silence till Susan had read the whole document in front of her. The interpreter looked at them when he finished.

'What do you think? Do you understand what this document says?'

'Are we free?' Hakim asked with a heavy accent.

'You certainly are, Mr Ahmed. You have been accepted and have been given refugee status. That means you can leave the hostel and move into temporary accommodation. You can look for work. You have the same rights as a British citizen. In five years, you can apply to settle in the UK. Congratulations.'

Hakim looked at Nazreen and they hugged each other tightly. Now they were free. Free to start their new life. Free to go where they pleased. Nazreen wiped tears from her eyes. 'Thank you, thank you, thank you.' She stood up and hugged the interpreter and case worker one after the other. She kissed their hands and bowed her head, her hands folded over her heart. Hakim did the same. Susan looked embarrassed.

'I will give you a leaflet with all the information about housing and claiming benefits,' she said.

'I don't want any benefits,' Hakim said. 'I want to work.'

'Not a problem,' Susan replied. 'You will have to apply for a National Insurance number. All the information is in the leaflet I've given you.'

Nazreen looked at the interpreter. 'Can we go anywhere we want? I made a friend here from Pakistan who's going to get married and she'll be living with her family near Manchester. Can we go there too?' she asked him.

'You can go wherever you want,' he said. 'This is a free country. I wish you all the best.' He stood up. 'Don't lose these documents. They're very important.'

Nazreen took the documents and held them tightly to her chest. 'I need to find Mariam and tell her the good news,' she said and ran out of the room. She skipped and jumped all the way back to the room. Her eyes sparkled with joy and Hakim pulled her in his arms and kissed her passionately. The documents sailed silently to the floor along with them.

'We've made it, Nazreen. Can you believe it? I'm so happy. Don't you want to stay here? There'll be so many opportunities for me to work here in the capital. They say the north is cold.'

'But Hakim, they'll put us in one of those tall tower blocks. Jasmin showed me round her flat and I didn't like it. It reminds me of this hostel with the luxury of an added bathroom. I want to be in the countryside. Mariam showed me a picture of her husband's house and garden. It's beautiful. I want to grow vegetables like my mother. You can work anywhere, Hakim. Please can we leave?'

How could he refuse her? She'd stuck by him all these months, endured hardship and interrogations. She blossomed into a beautiful, confident and happy woman in front of his eyes. Anyway, he'd promised her the earth. *Inshallah.*

39.

They travelled to the north by train with a loan given to them by the help organisation. Social Services had found temporary accommodation in a town called Oldham. She laughed with him when he said he didn't really want to live in a place that was called 'old ham'. Large areas of the town were populated by Bangladeshi and Pakistani communities who settled there in the 60s and 70s. Hakim hoped that they would blend in. Mariam's husband found him a job helping in a grocery shop not far from the flat he was now able to afford himself. Nazreen attended evening classes to learn Maths and English. After five years they applied for permanent residency and when it was granted, he had made one more trip back to Damascus, where he exchanged the gold and jewellery for cash, closed the bank account and smuggled the money, his uniform and his gun back to the UK. It had been a risk and he didn't know why he took the uniform and the gun. It could've been the end of him. These were things from his past that didn't have a place in his future, but he couldn't let go. He bought the grocery shop where he'd worked and they moved into the flat above.

He leased an allotment for Nazreen so she could sit in the sun. He built Nazreen a shed, where she could sit and look out of an imaginary window, onto an imaginary landscape. He'd thoughtfully painted a desert scene for Nazreen. It was not an oil painting and didn't turn out like he had imagined it in his head but when she saw it for the first time, she clapped her hands in happiness and kissed him passionately. They spent many evenings on the couch, looking at the stars illuminating the dark ceiling, at the sun, turning into a moon and recalled the time they spent in the desert. He should have burnt the uniform then and thrown the gun in the river behind the allotment but he could not part with it. He buried the uniform under the shed instead. It was a reminder to be a better man, to atone for his violent past.

Nazreen told him that she missed Iraq more than she thought possible. She even missed the heat, the sandstorms and the dirt. Deep in her heart she lived in hope and never gave up on the idea that, one day, they would return to the country of their birth. One day when Saddam was dead. They tried to start a family and after many years of trying she took him to a specialist. He was infertile. The doctor said it could be through exposure to the chemicals used in the Iran war. He was devastated. Nazreen held him close that night when he cried in her arms. It was Allah's wish.

'We still have each other,' she said to him and hugged him closer.

They lived a happy life in their neighbourhood for many years. They lived alongside their neighbours and he employed a young Pakistani boy who helped him translate. His customers were friendly people and he often watched Nazreen talking to the women in their broken English. They tried to fit in and the streets, with the shop windows full of Asian clothes, halal butchers, barbers and food outlets reminded him of Baghdad. Sometimes, when he took her out for a meal to a Persian restaurant in the city, smelling the lamb, infused with lemons and herbs from the kitchen, he was reminded of Iraq.

One night, in late April 2001, a seventy-six-year-old man was mugged and terribly beaten by three Asian males. The old man's mangled face was plastered all over the local paper and the national 'gutter' press picked up on the story the next day. They ignored the fact that justice was demanded by all communities, including the Asian but 'Whites beware' and 'Beaten for being white' were the slogans printed on the front of the newspapers that were delivered to his shop.

The event and the consequences highlighted society's shortcomings in many parts of the country. It highlighted the segregation and poverty in many towns. There was a great belief that more money was spent on the needs of Asian communities rather than British ones. There had been 'no go' areas for a long time, where Asians didn't go and vice versa. It was the perfect opportunity for the British National Party and National Front to spread hate and drum up support for their cause. *Look what these Asian thugs are doing to our World War Two veterans? They come to our country, ignore the way we live and expect to get away with it.* Those were their slogans.

Far right groups quickly tried to organize themselves and seize the moment but the councils denied permission to march through the town.

Instead, they infiltrated with football supporters from a visiting club and deliberately walked through multi-racial neighbourhoods, chanting racist slogans. National Front supporters arrived in town, clashing with members of the Anti-Nazi League and Asian groups. Like a seesaw, the situation escalated.

One weekend in late May two young males, one white, one Asian started a fight which soon got out of hand. A gang of white men attacked an Asian business. They threw a stone through a residential window. The heavily pregnant Asian woman inside was frightened to death. In retaliation, the aptly named pub 'Live and Let Live', was firebombed with the people still inside. They nearly died because their escape at the back was blocked. The government and the mosque elders pleaded for calm but it was too late and the anger spilled over into neighbouring Asian communities in Bradford and Leeds.

Hakim pulled the shutters of his shop down just in time. He looked through the blinds of the window in their flat above and saw riot police clashing with a wave of Asian youths trying to push them back down the road. The mob was throwing petrol bombs, bricks and bottles at the rows of police officers, holding their riot shields high for protection. The police tried hard to keep them under control. Hakim shouted for Nazreen and found her cowering in a corner of their bathroom, too scared to move. He had to pick her off the cold floor and carry her into the living room. He sat her on the couch and draped a blanket round her shivering body. They sat together in darkness all night, listening to the angry crowd outside. They had nowhere else to go. It died down for a while in the morning but as soon as it got dark, the rioting started again.

They were trapped in their flat for three days. Nazreen told him later that it reminded her of the day her father was taken and her mother had died.

'Is there a difference in this country? Are they coming to arrest us soon?' she asked him.

'Nazreen,' he said and held her by her shoulders. 'This country doesn't arrest people off the street, killing them. They have laws in this country and the police are here to uphold these laws. Don't be frightened. Nothing is going to happen to us. It'll be over soon.' He tried to assure her that she was safe but fetched his gun and hid it in the kitchen cupboard just in case. Nazreen felt uncomfortable to leave the house after calm had been restored and would not visit the allotment from that moment onwards.

He, on the other hand, needed the allotment.

He needed it as a memento of the past he left behind, a reminder that he was becoming a better man. Sitting on top of the uniform, looking at Nazreen and remembering the promise he made, made him work harder just like he promised Allah on the trip through the desert in Iraq and the journey through the mountains of Syria. He thought he had become a better man. He attended prayers every day, given hundreds of pounds to charities over the years and was involved in an Organisations for Integration. He helped fill vans with donations, delivering aid to Syria's refugees. He tried so hard to make up for his wrongdoings and she loved him for it. Now, the uniform was to become his undoing.

How could he survive without that love?

He would have had a chance of true redemption, if only he could have given her a child. He'd convinced himself that it was Allah's punishment. He couldn't give her a child and he had kept quiet about the only child she ever had, let her believe the baby had died when he could've told her that she was alive. Her wish to return to the country of her birth had been the hardest to grant and they had many discussions but, in the end, he would sell the business and they were going to return to Iraq. Now, that was impossible.

Soon, she would find out what he had done. Soon, the whole world would know how he had tortured and executed in the name of Saddam. He followed orders but in the eyes of the world that was not going to make a difference; it couldn't be an excuse and everybody had to stand to be accounted one day. The possibility of deportation and standing trial, which would end in a prison sentence or even death, didn't grieve him as much as losing her love. He couldn't let that happen. He pushed his chair back from the table.

'I'm making a cup of tea,' he said, went into the kitchen and pulled a packet out of his trouser pocket. He crushed the sleeping tablets with the back of a spoon and stirred the water in the teapot, till the powder dissolved.

'Strong and sweet, just as you like it,' he said when he returned to the living room. He poured her a cup and handed it to her.

'Lovely,' she said blowing on the hot liquid. 'Just what I need, you do look after me, don't you?' she smiled her beautiful smile.

'Drink while it's still hot,' he said and watched her as she finished her cup.

'I'm tired,' she whispered a little while later and with tears in his eyes he lowered her body down on the couch and placed her head on a cushion, gently covering her body with a blanket.

'You go to sleep now, *Habibi*. I'm right behind you.' He hugged her close to him one last time.

'I won't be long.' He kissed his wife goodbye and pushed the hair from her face one last time. 'I love you.' He hardly heard the words. Her hand tried to reach for his but it flopped to the side. He picked it up, kissed her fingers lovingly and tucked her hand back under the blanket.

'I love you more,' he replied and sat back in his chair opposite her. With tears streaming down his face he watched Nazreen slowly pass into unconsciousness. He got up and poured the tea down the sink. Cleaned the cups and put them on the draining board. He went downstairs into the shop, opened the safe under the cash register and pulled out his gun.

'Till death parts us,' he said to her sleeping body and sat back in his chair. 'May Allah be merciful and let me find you in paradise.'

Did he redeem himself enough in the eyes of Allah? Would he be forgiven? He wondered as he lifted the gun to his head, pulling the trigger.

40.

Amal sat quietly in a corner and reflected on her day. So much misery and heartbreak. She didn't know how these human shells could ever recover after the torment they had endured.

She had seen enough misery in her own short lifetime to understand a human's desire to survive at any cost.

Life had become even harder after Saddam Hussein's execution in December 2006. The daily suicide bombings and civil war had taken its toll on her father, who tried hard to make a living as a taxi driver. He had been replaced in favour of another teacher and could not return to work. Her mother was ill and needed medicine. The sanctions, that were meant to press the government into submission and the people to revolt, had been in place since forever but they were hurting the poorest people of Iraq.

The former palaces and abandoned government buildings of Saddam Hussein had become the focal point of the American occupation. Most houses of the former government district in the heart of Baghdad were now isolated, surrounded by barriers. They named it the 'Green Zone' because of the lush green parks surrounding the area. It had been surreal when her father took her there one day to look for a job. They stood in line for hours under the blazing sun with hundreds of other people, just as desperate as them, in front and behind, without water or shelter. The soldiers with their guns, wearing helmets and flak jackets scared her; they seemed nervous and kept pointing their guns at the people queuing in line, ready to fire into the crowd at any moment.

She was surprised at how quiet it was once they were cleared by the soldiers at the checkpoint. Saddam's monument of the two crossing swords held by his hands looked untouched by the fighting. She looked up at the swords crossing above her head and wondered why it was still there.

The lush gardens were in stark contrast to the smelly streets and the hustle and bustle outside the compound. It was very peaceful. She could hear birds tweeting in the palm trees, fighting for dates. She didn't want to leave and wished they had been clever enough to occupy one of the empty houses that were left abandoned by the former government officials. She heard that a lot of homeless people had managed to occupy these houses before the Americans closed the district off. She imagined being in one of those houses, sitting on the terrace, sipping lemonade and jumping into the pool when the sun got too hot. She told her father after they left the compound and he had laughed.

'They will be living like rats, honey, life won't be any different for them apart from having a roof over their heads.'

Back on the streets outside the compound the fear for their lives returned almost instantly. Her father held her hand and moved her closer to his body. Lawlessness still dominated everyday life. People got mugged and shot but nobody seemed to do anything about it. She kept her head down, following her father closely and never looked anybody in the eyes. More frightening than walking with her father, who was able to give her some sort of protection, was walking to the market with her mother to shop for groceries. She concluded one day that it didn't really matter where you were in the country, death could come at any minute.

Suicide bombers were not only targeting American soldiers and military checkpoints, they would explode themselves on buses, in mosques and schools. They targeted the markets and bazaars. They drove vehicles into busy crowds and onto bridges where there was no room to escape. They would wear suicide vests underneath their clothes on buses, looking like ordinary people going about their business and detonate their deathly load. It happened every day. She didn't forget her father's face when he heard about a suicide bomber who blew his vehicle up in Baghdad's Sadriyah market, killing 135 people and wounding 305. Just in the month of February, 463 people died and 632 were wounded. It was at the end of that month when her father turned to her mother.

'There is nothing left for us here. The Iraq I loved is dead. It has been blown apart.' And one rainy day in May 2007 her father packed them and their belongings into his clapped-out taxi and they drove over the border to Syria.

41.

Amal was sixteen at the time and eager to learn. Her dream was to be an independent woman and for a future in a free country. She wanted to be useful and make a difference in the world. It was impossible in Iraq.

'You will see Amal,' her father said, driving the car over the dusty highway. 'Everything is going to be much better. The Assad government is reforming the country. The people elected him president and they love him for it. Don't you think that is progress? Did you know that his wife Asma travelled the country and spoke to the people of Syria to see what could be done better in the future? Can you believe that a woman could do that? She supports women's rights and an equal education. You will love it there. You are going to become a doctor after all,' he said after a while, took his hand of the steering wheel and squeezed her fingers. He'd been so excited.

She remembered the night they arrived in Damascus very well. They couldn't drive the car any further and had to stop because of a huge crowd gathering in the streets. Her father stayed behind in the car with her mother, who was frightened but Amal opened the window and climbed onto the roof. The people of Damascus were lining the streets, celebrating Bashar Assad's re-election win. It was a landslide win and nobody questioned the only candidate on the ballot paper.

There were thousands of people on the main square, all wearing white T-shirts with their president's image on the front. The side streets were flooded with people laughing and shouting Assad's name, carrying his picture, waving flags. And because nobody was frightened of the men waving their guns in the air, Amal wasn't either. They slept in the car that night once the celebrations died down and arrived at her mother's cousin's house the next day.

It was cramped and she had to share a room with four other children but that didn't matter to her. She started school and soon became one of the best pupils in her class. The desire for knowledge drove her to be the best in every subject. It was difficult to study in the house with all the screaming and goings on. She found a peaceful space on the roof of the building and her life in Iraq seemed to be millions of miles away.

Her poorly mum never recovered and took a turn for the worst. She passed away quietly one night, which left her father and Amal heartbroken. After the funeral her father found a small teaching post near Damascus and three years later Amal passed her nursing exams with distinction. Her mother would have been so proud. She applied for a scholarship and was ecstatic when she was given a place at Damascus University.

They shared a flat on the outskirts of the city with another family by then and her father drove a taxi at night to boost his meagre wage to support her dream of becoming a doctor.

She began her studies in 2010. One day in December a friend showed her a picture of a man in Tunisia setting himself on fire. He could not take the injustice any more and hoped to set a sign against the corruption in the Tunisian government. The public was enraged and demanded for the Tunisian president to resign. The protestors took to the streets and the Tunisian government was overthrown in January.

The demonstrations spilled over into Egypt and thousands of demonstrators gathered in Tahrir Square demanding the resignation of their president Hosni Mubarak. Like a tsunami that couldn't be stopped, the wave of revolution spilled into Libya towards the regime of Muammar Gaddafi, starting a civil war. The rebel forces captured Tripoli, overthrowing Gaddafi's regime. Gaddafi was killed in October. She saw his death on the Internet. Although she was glad the dictator was dead, the images of his last moments, bloodied and beaten, made her sick to her stomach. The foreign media called it the 'Arab Rising'.

'How much longer is it going to be till the trouble is going to arrive on our doorstep?' Amal asked herself and put down the *Vogue* magazine, portraying the first lady as a revolutionary thinker. She carried on going to school.

In April the media reported the death of a thirteen-year-old boy in Daraa. He had been arrested in a rally. He accompanied his family to protest against the detention and torture of twenty-three of his fellow pupils. The graffiti on their school gates read *It's your turn next, Doctor*, referring to Assad. The boy had been arrested and tortured. When his dead body had been returned to his family, he was covered in cigarette burns and his genitals had been cut off. It sparked outrage, resulting in a peaceful protest of thousands of people in the streets of Daraa, asking the government to arrest the culprits.

Everything could have been different that day but the government responded with violence which resulted in the death of hundreds of people. It also triggered the uprising of hundreds of thousands of people all over the country.

One evening Amal returned to the flat to find her father sitting in front of the television, staring into space.

'What is the matter?' she had asked, putting her books down on the table.

'It will come to nothing,' he replied looking at the television.

'They will suffer, like we've suffered all these years in Iraq. Nobody seems to learn from the past. It just keeps repeating itself. Governments fighting wars on the backs of innocent people.' He put his head in his hands and rubbed his face in despair.

'Enough is enough,' he said and looked up at her. 'I will not sit and watch another life being destroyed, destroyed by violence and men.'

Again, he'd packed her in the car and this time, they fled over the border to Turkey.

42.

There was nothing much to do in the refugee camp. She watched, as hundreds of people arrived from Aleppo and other parts of the country every day. Some of them were lucky, they managed to bring some of their belongings, others just had the clothes on their backs. Men, women and children of all ages, the elderly and the sick, brought on makeshift stretchers, carts and wheelbarrows. They were dusty, hungry and dehydrated, a lot of them injured by flying shrapnel, bricks and mortar. Etched on their faces was an unbelievable sadness. She could still see the terror in their eyes. That look would stay with her forever.

The people kept on coming. Day after day. Night after night. The world looked on in horror. Help organisations tried to do everything in their power to deal with the exodus. It simply would not stop. Hundreds, no, thousands of tents had been erected so far, and still they kept coming. Foreign governments offered to grant refugee status to some of them. These were the lucky ones. Others were simply hoping to return to their homes.

'Which homes?' she sometimes asked herself.

Some people vanished. One day they were in their tents, the next day they were gone. She heard that people who had the financial means walked to the coast or got picked up by trucks to be shipped to Europe. Who could blame them? The camps were holding facilities of human misery. It was loud, overcrowded and smelled worse than a rubbish tip. Human waste filled the gaps between the tents when it rained. Children were playing in the dirty water and became ill. Stray cats and dogs were fighting over the scraps left out on the walkways and she heard rats rummaging outside the tents. Pregnant women who gave birth were lucky to keep their infants alive. The aid that was shipped in would be distributed but a lot of the goods would simply vanish to be sold on the black market for a profit. Who would want to bring up a child in these conditions?

'This is better than to die at home being shot at and bombed,' one of the women told her. She'd fled her home in Aleppo. The wall of the building she lived in with her four children collapsed onto the street below after a mortar hit the side. They waited two days to be rescued during a break in the shelling. For those two days they had prayed for Allah's mercy. They were left with no water or food in the room overlooking the street below, left in fear that the rest of the building would crumble and bury them under the rest of the flats above. She'd never been more frightened in her life.

She didn't care about what she was leaving behind. Her home, her parents, her friends. She just wanted to get out and live in peace. Have a chance to see her children grow up in a place where nobody would hate so much that they were trying to kill them. She'd lost her baby to dysentery the day before and clutched the remaining three in her arms. She said this with tears streaming down her face, the children looking up at her lost and sad, their faces covered in dust, tired from the long walk to the border.

'I will do anything, you understand? Anything, not to go back to that place.'

Amal had left the family to grieve in peace, feeling hollow and in despair, her heart hurt and she felt desperate to help. She needed to feel useful and started to volunteer in one of the MSF tents. She was a qualified nurse after all.

They welcomed her with open arms. She was the go-between for the people arriving and the medical staff, translating the questions the doctors asked and the patients' answers. She helped bandage the wounds left by the war and the walk along the dusty desert road. There were long hours but she never faltered. For the first time in her life she felt like she was in control of her own destiny.

One day, a man entered the tent she was working in with a severely dehydrated child in his arms. The boy had been injured by a bullet. Luckily, his mother had pushed him forward so the bullet had just scraped his body, but he landed on his face and had passed out. They were going to put him on a drip and tend to the cuts on his face. As she tried to find a vein for the saline drip, she caught the man looking at her. She smiled.

'My name is Tom,' he said.

'Nice to meet you,' she replied. 'Now step back please so I can tend to this boy.' He turned on his heels and continued bringing in the wounded. She saw a lot more of Tom after that.

Wherever she worked, he must've found an excuse to be near. Passing her gauze when she was changing a patient's dressing or handing her a new bag of saline to exchange the old one. One day, they met by the little boy's bedside.

'He's recovering well?' She looked up from her patient.

'He's doing fine. No fever. I think we can let his mum know, so she can take him out of here.'

Tom was taller than her, in fact, he towered over her like a giant. He had kind eyes, which were piercing blue as she later discovered. He had blond curly hair, which fell to his shoulders, but was kept in a ponytail. His shoulders were wide and his body was pure muscle; he clearly worked out. His smile dazzled her.

'Care for some lunch?'

43.

After the first lunch, they had more lunches, sometimes dinner in his canteen. He was a doctor and fresh out of university he decided to volunteer for a year with the MSF (Médecins Sans Frontières). He said it felt it was his duty to help. He told her about his life and she shared hers with him. She had been nervous to introduce him to her father as he was not a Muslim, but her worries were unfounded. The two men would sit outside the tent on plastic chairs, playing chess or just in silence, enjoying each other's company after a long day.

When Tom thought they were alone, he had held her hand and kissed her on the lips. She'd never felt anything so strong in her entire life, she didn't want it to stop.

One day, he had borrowed a Land Rover and they had driven out of camp, away from the noise and the smell. He'd brought a picnic basket with him and laid a blanket on the floor under a tree that had not yet been felled for firewood. They were sitting close together, their backs against the bark, watching the sun set over the horizon.

'You know I've fallen in love with you, don't you?' he said taking one of her hands.

She nodded. 'I've only known you for a few months, Amal. I know this seems to be wrong but I feel that after what we see every day, life is too short to hang around and wait for the perfect moment. I've not got much to my name but what I have I want to share with you. Will you marry me?' She looked at him in surprise and pretended to think about his question for a minute.

'Yes,' she said. 'I feel the exact same. I love you too from the bottom of my heart. I will marry you but first we have to speak to my father.' He took her hand and put a piece of string round her finger. Their eyes met and he kissed her gently on the lips.

'I'm sorry that I haven't got a proper ring for you but there is nowhere I could buy one!' he said apologetically.

'I don't care, my love, as long as you are with me, I don't need anything else.'

They tied the knot, having been granted special permission, in the British Embassy in Ankara, two month later. Her father stayed behind on the camp. He was in the middle of opening a school for the children with the help of UNICEF and said they needed him more than her. She had been sad but he had given her a little box before she climbed into the car.

'I promised your mother to give this to you when you get married. She would have been so proud of you. I'm proud of you.' He kissed her forehead.

'When you return, we will talk.' She didn't know what he wanted to talk about and before she could ask the car set off.

Now, on her honeymoon, she sat on a beach on Lesbos, one of the Greek Islands, happier than she could ever have imagined. But, yet again, she had witnessed another human tragedy this morning while they were out on an early morning walk, they rescued people from a boat that had landed on the shores. It seemed that she couldn't escape her responsibility to help other human beings wherever she went.

Amal felt the box her father had given her in her jacket pocket. She nearly forgot it was there and took it out. She turned the box in her hands and untied the knot. She opened the lid.

Inside the box was a bracelet, red-gold and tiny, as if made for a baby. She lifted it from the box and looked at it closely. She could make out two names and a year. Mohamed and Nazreen, 1987. When Tom returned to her with a bottle of water, she handed him the bracelet.

'What do you think this means?'

He looked at it closely and shrugged his shoulders. 'You have to ask your father when we return to the camp. Maybe that's what he meant when he said he needed to talk on your return.'

'Come on, Amal,' and he reached for her hand to pull her up off the floor. 'It's our honeymoon. Let's find a spot where there are less people.'

The rest of the week they spent in a blissful bubble, far away from all the misery and worry. They only had eyes for each other. They enjoyed each other's company. They went for long walks on the beach, visited the ancient sites and took a boat trip to a deserted beach where they swam naked in the clear blue water of the Mediterranean and made love with a deep and quiet passion on the warm sand, with only the sound of the waves for company. She never felt so loved in her life and regretted every minute he was away from her, even if it was only to fetch some olives from the breakfast buffet.

On the last afternoon of their stay, they were cuddled up together on a hammock, suspended between two olive trees at the edge of the water. The sun shone through the branches and let the leaves shine silver in the light breeze from the sea; the water was lapping on the sand in a rhythmic chime that made them sleepy and relaxed. His phone interrupted the silence with a loud buzzing noise. They both sat up, startled.

'It's my mother,' he said, knowing that she would never ring unless it was important, he put her on screen.

'Hi, Mum, how's Devon? How are you? Is anything the matter?' After they listened to his mother explaining her extraordinary phone call, he hung up and looked at Amal.

She looked to be in shock. They boarded the plane back to Turkey. Amal needed to speak to her father desperately. There were so many unanswered questions.

44.

The Herald

Police discovered the bodies of two people earlier this morning in a flat in the Whitfield area of town. Mr Aktar from the legal firm, Aktar and Sons called the police, concerned for the couple's welfare.

'I was supposed to meet the Ahmeds at their house at eight o'clock this morning for the sale of his business. I knocked on the door and I phoned but there was no answer. It's tragic. I don't think they have any family in the UK.'

The man was pronounced dead at the scene. His wife has been taken to hospital. She is described as serious but stable.

The police are treating this incident as an attempted murder-suicide and are not looking for a third party. The inquiry is ongoing.

Anybody with information regarding this incident should ring 101 or contact their local police station.

45.

She found her father sitting on a rug in front of his tent.

'I need to speak with you, *Baba*,' she said without formally greeting him. He looked up at them and seeing the panic in his daughter's eyes patted the space on the carpet next to him.

'Sit down you two and I will answer as truly as I can.'

She lowered herself to the ground, looking at her father expectantly. She opened her rucksack and handed him the little box.

'What can you tell me about this and who are the people inscribed on the inside?' she asked.

He took the box from her hands and looked at the bracelet's inscription.

'This is yours, Amal. It was the only thing you had with you when a soldier found you in the desert in 1991.' She inhaled sharply to say something, Tom put a hand on her arm.

'Let him speak, honey,' he said.

'Your mother, well, the woman you thought was your mother, made me swear not to tell you, till you were married. She hoped that you would understand one day.' Glancing into the distance, focusing on a point in the past her father started to talk.

'We couldn't have children, you see, we tried but Allah did not bless our marriage. We stayed with family in Basra when the war broke out. The war was terrible but didn't last very long. Shortly after the ceasefire, Saddam's government troops started crushing the rebellion. In March I read an article in the Basra paper that the Red Crescent was looking for the relatives of a baby girl, found in the desert by a British soldier, parents presumed dead.

'"Why should the poor child be without parents?" your mother said to me. "We could be her parents, we can take her back to Baghdad, nobody will know. God wants us to look after her and love her, that's why we are here. What kind of mother leaves her baby to die in the desert anyway? She doesn't deserve her."

'I didn't argue with your mother, she was usually right.

'We decided to take a chance. I spoke to the imam after prayers and he made inquiries at the Red Crescent headquarters; nobody had claimed you for their own. I will never forget the look on your mother's face when she held you in her arms. We loved you from the first moment. It was very chaotic times back then and nobody checked our credentials. The nurses had called you Hope, we called you Amal. Two languages, same meaning.

'The bracelet you wore when you were found, was probably your mother's. We tried to find out what had happened to her over the years but it was too difficult, as you can imagine.

'We tried our best and loved you as if you were our own flesh and blood. Sometimes I think we loved you more because you were a gift from Allah. I've always tried to do right by you. Your mother was so proud of you but she thought you would stop loving us if you knew the secret of your birth.' He looked at his hands in his lap and fell silent. That was the longest speech she had heard from him in a long time.

Amal took her father's hands in hers.

'You've been the best parents a girl could ever want, *Baba*. I love you.' She kissed him on both cheeks and hugged him tight.

'Thank you for everything you have ever done for me. You are the only parents I've ever known and I love you very much. You allowed me to grow to be the woman that I am.' She sat back and took Tom's hand. Pouring more tea from the pot she turned back to her father.

'*Baba*, Tom's mum rang yesterday while we were still in Greece. She read a newspaper article to us because she recognised yours and mother's names in it. She wondered if there was a connection.'

Her father leant back into the cushions and looked at her with surprise in his eyes. 'It is all over Facebook and Twitter. There is a campaign in England to find the girl abandoned in the desert.' She looked from her father to her husband and back to her father.

'I would really like to meet this soldier who rescued me. Do you think that would be possible?'

46.

Tom had been in touch with the newspaper and they arranged a visa for Amal and a flight to England. On board, all Amal could think about was meeting the soldier who saved her life. She owed him so much. She looked at Tom next to her, reading a paper. He showed her the front page and pointed at a picture.

'Look, it's you.'

She examined the picture closer. It showed a soldier holding a baby to the camera.

'I was so tiny,' she said. 'Do you think I was premature? I must've had a guardian angel that night, *Mashallah*. I was very, very lucky. I would have liked it better if my father could have come with us,' she said. She was sad to leave her father behind but he could not get a visa in time.

'I'm so excited to meet your mum, Tom. I feel quite sick. I have only spoken to your mother via Skype and FaceTime till now. I still have to wait another two days to meet her. I wish she would be waiting for us at the airport. Do you think she will like me?'

'She will adore you, sweetheart, what's there not to like?'

Tom looked at his wife. She reminded him of a flower he saw when he first arrived in the camp. Growing amongst the tents between all the devastation and chaos, despite of the relentless heat and freezing cold, its head was turned towards the sun, absorbing life. That was Amal. He took her hand and gazed into her dark bottomless eyes, surrounded by thick, black lashes. 'Most girls would die for lashes like that,' he thought to himself and he kissed her softly on both lids.

'You are the best thing that's ever happened to me and my mother will love you, just like I love you.' She kissed him back and settled her head on his shoulders. For the first time in her life she felt truly content.

The plane landed at Manchester Airport in the early hours of the morning. The newspaper had sent a car to pick them up. She felt a little dazzled with all the attention but fell straight asleep, once her head hit the fluffy pillow. It was nearly dawn when she woke, disorientated with the unfamiliar surroundings she slowly opened her eyes. She felt for his body next to her and moved closer. Still lulled in his warmth she heard the birds greeting the morning sun in the trees beneath her window. She slipped out from underneath the covers and opened the drapes to let in the sun. She opened the window and sat on the window sill. Feeling the sunlight on her face she closed her eyes and inhaled the sweet scent of the morning breeze. She heard him rise and moments later he wrapped his arms around her, kissing her on the nape of her neck.

'Can't you sleep, sweetheart?' he asked. 'It's only five o'clock. Come back to bed.'

'Not yet,' she said. 'I'm enjoying the peace and quiet. I'm too excited to go back to sleep.'

'You call this racket peace and quiet? I forgot how loud the birds can be in the morning. And anyway, who said I want to go back to sleep?' he said with a smile.

They were going to meet with the journalist after breakfast. The waiters had stared at her at first: she put on the dress she wore when she got married. They had not seen a more exotic, naturally beautiful woman, in this part of Cheshire in a while. They pulled out a chair for her and called her 'Ma'am', she was terribly embarrassed. Nobody ever called her ma'am before.

'I should have worn jeans and a T-shirt,' she said. 'They're staring at me as if they never seen a woman in a dress before,' she complained.

'They're expecting to meet a desert rose, honey, and that's what they'll get,' Tom replied with his mouth full of food. He continued to tuck into his 'full English' breakfast. It looked like he had not eaten in days. She nibbled on a croissant and sipped her tea.

A man appeared in the doorway and rushed to her side.

'You,' and he took Amal's hand without asking. 'You made big headlines in this country. Your story is in every newspaper up and down the country and we feel privileged that you want to talk to us first, exclusively.'

He walked around the table and shook Tom's hand. 'I'm Patrick. Lovely to meet you.'

'I must say. You look wonderful, Amal, can I call you Amal? Like a princess straight from *Arabian Nights*. Lovely, just lovely. Can I have a cup please, waiter?' he said, snipping his finger in the air.

'This is what's happening today,' the journalist rattled on. 'We are going to take the car to town where we will meet the Montgomerys. They are just as excited to see you. The meeting will take place in a private function room.

'We've arranged a photo opportunity for other interested magazines and such after the meeting. I'm sure you find this a bit overwhelming at present but I assure you that you don't need to be frightened. The people of Manchester have been waiting for this moment for a while. Let's not let them wait any longer.'

They made the short journey into town. She clutched Tom's arm as if she was going to drown. Her heart raced and her palms were wet with perspiration. She wiped them on the seat of the car, hoping that nobody noticed her nervousness.

The car stopped round the back of a building and the driver slid the door open to let her get out. She followed the journalist and her husband up the stairs. 'This is too much,' she thought and needed to steady herself, holding onto the railings tightly. She hesitated. Tom looked over his shoulder and rushed immediately to her side.

'Are you OK?' he asked concerned.

'I'm fine.' She smiled. 'It's not like I'm going to my execution, is it?' He smiled at her encouragingly and took her hand.

They arrived at a double door. The man knocked and entered the room. She had been so nervous about this meeting but when she entered the room and stepped out from behind her husband's back, a very handsome, bearded older man walked towards her in a few big strides. He carried a huge smile on his face and took her hand in both of his.

'Hello again,' he said beaming. 'Long time no seen, girl,' he said and pulled her into an embrace, kissing her on both cheeks. Then he held her further away, not letting go of her hands.

'Let's have a proper look at you then, see if it was worth saving you.'

He looked her up and down, whistled and glanced at Tom. 'Not bad, lad, not bad at all,' he said with a wink and a smile in his direction.

Inga had been hovering in the background. Now, she ushered herself forward and grabbed Jonathan's sleeve.

'Hi.' She pulled her husband to one side towards Tom and extended her hand, thought better of it and engulfed Amal in a big hug. She planted a kiss on each cheek.

'I have been waiting for this moment for such a long time. It's such a pleasure to meet you in person, at last.' She turned around to Tom and extended her arms for a hug. 'You must be the husband. Welcome back.'

Still a bit shaken Amal sat at the table. Inga sat herself next to Amal and took her hand. 'Isn't it just wonderful,' she kept repeating. 'How small this world really is.

'Extraordinary. Don't you think?'

'She's a bit overwhelmed at the moment, Mrs Montgomery,' Tom said. 'She's not normally this quiet.'

'Please call me Inga. Of course, she is. How stupid of me. Come on, let's eat. Life is better with a slice of cake, isn't it, Jon?'

They drank tea out of tiny porcelain cups and ate little sandwiches and cakes from beautifully decorated stands. Amal felt very special. Clutching at the chain on her neck, she pulled the little bangle out from underneath her dress.

'Do you remember seeing this when you found me?' she asked Jonathan.

'I don't recall,' he said, 'but it was a lifetime ago. It all happened so fast and my only concern was to get you to a medic! Those were desperate times back then and I couldn't wait to get back to my unit.'

'Are you sure you didn't see my mother and father?' She looked sad.

'I didn't, love. I'm sorry. We did a thorough search of the area the day before and buried the bodies we discovered. There was nobody else in the vicinity of the burnt-out tank. I looked around again after I delivered you to the medics. I found bloody cloth and the earth was disturbed behind the tank but there was no sign of human life. I wish I could tell you more, but I can't.' She sighed.

'I am forever grateful to you,' she said after a while. 'You saved my life and without you I would have died out there. I would never have met Tom.' She took his hand.

'It was fate, the night you found me, it was fate when you discovered the bag under the shed. God works in mysterious ways.'

'Actually,' Inga intervened, 'I found the bag, and I talked to Patrick and got the ball rolling. Jon might be the hero in all this but I can't let him take all the credit.'

Jonathan patted her on the knee. 'We know, Miss Marple.' They all laughed apart from Amal.

'Who is Miss Marple? A relative?' she asked, which made them laugh even harder.

Patrick stood up and reminded them of the photo opportunity for the reporters waiting outside. They got up. Jonathan muttered something under his breath, Inga straightened her make-up and hair. Amal and Tom flanked by Jonathan and Inga, stepped out onto the terrace.

'You're enjoying this, Inga, aren't you?' Jonathan smiled at his wife.

'It's like winning the lottery,' she replied. 'Only better.'

They were exhausted. The cameras had snapped and Inga, Jonathan and Amal answered a hundred questions from the reporters. It was all a bit too much.

Inga and Jonathan accompanied them back to the hotel in the tranquil Cheshire countryside. Before Patrick left, he took Inga to one side.

'I was going to speak to you earlier but didn't get a chance. I found the man who leased your allotment before Wilfred. He was called Mohamed Ahmed but when I asked him two days ago, he denied ever knowing about the uniform. He said the shed was already there. I looked up his name in the national records and he and his wife were granted citizenship in 1995. His wife's called Nazreen.'

Inga drew a sharp breath. 'Could it really be her? You'll need to speak to him again, Patrick,' she said. 'Make sure his wife is with him.'

'Well,' he replied. 'That might be a little difficult. He killed himself that same evening and tried to kill his wife with sleeping tablets.'

'Oh no, my dear sweet Jesus.' Inga put her hands in front of her mouth and looked at Amal.

'His wife survived and is cared for in hospital,' Patrick continued. 'The nurses wouldn't let me speak to her till she was off the critical list. She's left with some liver and kidney damage.'

'The poor woman. Isn't it just typical? He takes his own life but decides her fate for her. Despicable person. Do you think she could be THE Nazreen from the engraving?'

'It's possible,' Patrick said. 'I suppose there are many people with the name Mohamed but all the signs are there. Don't say anything just yet, Inga.' He shook her hand and left through the double doors.

They sat in front of the big screen in the television lounge. Tom and Jonathan nursing a pint, Inga with a large glass of wine, Amal sipped lemonade with a dash of lime.

'What a day this has been,' Amal said and sank back against the cushions.

'I hope Granada Television knows how to take a few pounds off my waistline,' Inga said and took a large gulp of her wine.

'The camera never lies, darling,' Jonathan replied, grinning at Tom, who winked back in response.

'I'll speak to you later.' Inga pulled a face, which made everybody laugh, apart from her. They listened intently as they watched themselves on the screen.

47.

In a hospital bed Nazreen stared out of the window. A television was showing the news but Nazreen was caught up in her own thoughts.

She didn't remember anything about that night. The last thing she remembered was Hakim telling her to drink her tea. She woke up in this hospital and the doctors said she was lucky to be alive.

'Lucky?' she'd asked the polite doctor standing at her bedside when she woke up. She didn't agree with him on that. Why had Hakim left her? He broke his promise. If he felt so strongly about not returning to Iraq, he could have told her. Why would he leave her all alone in this world? He should've made a proper job of it and shot her too. Why did he do it? Why? Why? Nazreen kept repeating the question in her head. Over and over. What did she do? Was it all her fault. It hurt so much.

When the police came to interview her, they couldn't answer her question either. Hakim didn't leave a note, no explanation. Nothing. The policeman left her sobbing hysterically and they had to give her a sedative.

A picture of a family appeared on the television screen on the wall and a young woman dressed like a princess pulled a necklace out of from under her dress and held a tiny bracelet to the lens of the camera. Nazreen reached for the remote and turned the volume up. She took a deep breath and sat up, frantically pressing the button on her bed fob.

When nobody came straight away, she tried to climb out of bed, pulling at the cannula, attaching her arm to a drip. She freed herself from the pulse monitor, which in turn set off the alarm.

Finally, nurses came running into her room. Nazreen kept pointing to the television and walked past the nurses towards the door with her hospital gown gaping at the back and blood dropping on the floor. The nurses tried to restrain her by her arms but she started clawing at their faces, shouting at them to let her go. Her language switched between Arabic and English. One of the doctors who came running in administered a sedative. Still pointing at the television, she sank back into her pillow and closed her eyes.

'I think she said "daughter",' one of the nurses said to her colleague, who felt for Nazreen's pulse.

'You must have misheard, Nora,' she said.

'When she was admitted the notes said she has no next of kin.' Nora shrugged her shoulders and bandaged the wound in Nazreen's hand.

48.

Autumn 2018

It's a beautiful early September evening. This year the forecasters had been right for a change. The promised heatwave went on and on, threatening a hosepipe ban at one point and everyone kept recalling the summer of 1976.

Amal watches Mr Montgomery, his name is Jonathan, she reminds herself, Tom and her father around the BBQ. Her father had been granted a temporary visa and arrived the previous day. They look like an odd trio. Her hero, Jonathan, beefy, in his shorts and rugby shirt, her father, in his best clothes looking from one man to the other and Tom, towering above them all. They're laughing at the dog, rolling around in one of the flower beds. Inga's grandchildren are playing in the sandpit. The gate opens and Inga's friend Libby pops her head around the corner, smiling and waving.

Amal waves back at her. 'How far we have come,' she says to herself. She turns around to the shed and grins. It was not an actual shed any more.

'Wilfred's turning in his grave,' Pete said to her earlier.

Inga had been very busy at instructing Jonathan to build her a large summer house with windows at either side of the doors. It's the biggest shed she's ever seen. It's built on the spot where Inga found the bag and the patio doors open out onto a vegetable garden built on various terraces. Fruit trees have been planted nearby and she can hear the trickle of the stream, running over the stones behind the fence. To the right, Inga had instructed to build a chicken shed, her hens all have names and are clucking happily.

As predicted, Inga ignored all the rules of shed painting and her summer house, or girl shed, as she calls it, is covered in a pale grey with dark, green frames around the windows and doors. There's a garland with colourful triangles moving in the warm evening breeze. Strings of red heart-shaped solar lights, that are going to light up when it got dark, dangle from the ceiling. The patio doors are open and inviting. Pete is smiling at her in passing, carrying a tray with refreshments for the men.

Amal joins the women on the sofa. They look at the mural a friend of Inga's has painted on the wall. It takes up most of the space and nobody could miss it. It is a painting of a desert landscape, sand dunes and palm trees are divided by an almighty river, boats seem to be moving upstream, with their white sails blowing in an imaginary wind.

'Are you comfortable, Ummi? Do you want me to get your shawl?' Nazreen turns to face her daughter.

'I am very, very happy. Thank you.'

Inga looks at both and smiles. After all Nazreen had to endure the last few weeks, Inga is happy to see her smile. Patrick, who left his telephone number, received a phone call from one of the nurses the day of the television broadcast. They rushed Amal to the hospital. It had been a very emotional reunion and everybody needed some time to come to terms with the events. Tom's mother arrived for support and stayed with them for Hakim's funeral.

A post mortem examination had been ordered by the coroner. On the day of the inquest the examiner told the coroner that Hakim had died from a single gunshot wound to the head. There wasn't a suicide note present when the police discovered the body. Patrick was questioned and re-told his meeting with Mohamed that morning. Nazreen had to give evidence as to the state of mind her husband seemed to be in on the evening of his death. With tears streaming down her face she told the court that he appeared to be his normal self that evening and the first lie.

'He was cleaning his gun at the time I fell asleep, your honour,' she said.

'Mrs Ahmed, you were found with a large dose of prescription painkillers in your system. Can you explain why he might have exceeded the recommended dose of the drug, putting your life in danger?'

'I can't, your honour. I think I had a migraine that evening and I asked him to give me a pain killer,' she lied. 'Maybe he didn't read the instructions properly. I can't think of a reason he would have deliberately tried to kill me. He loved me!' She broke down and had to be helped back to her seat.

'Ladies and gentlemen, Mrs Ahmed. After hearing all the evidence, I conclude that Mr Ahmed's death was accidental. I find him of sound mind on the evening of his demise. He didn't seem to be depressed nor did he have any money trouble. The police didn't find a suicide note. The witness stated that her husband was cleaning his gun when she fell asleep. The high amount of painkillers found in Mrs Ahmed's system could've been given to her accidently. I hereby declare Mr Ahmed's demise as death by misadventure.'

'The body will be released to you, Mrs Ahmed. I'm sorry for your loss.'

'I'm glad so many people came to pay their last respects. He was a good man and he was loved by many. I'm thankful but I'm glad that today is over.'

On the evening after Hakim's burial they all sat together in Nazreen's living room. Nazreen held her daughter's hand while she told the story of her forced marriage to Amal's father. How Hakim rescued her and their escape from Iraq. Inga showed her the newspaper clipping.

'I'm so sad that Hakim didn't have the courage to speak to me about Amal. He lied to me all these years. Why didn't he mention it, Amal? I would've forgiven him. We could have had all the time in the world to be a family. We could've had grandchildren.' She looked at the picture of him on her wall.

'I loved him more than life itself.'

'He must've had his reasons.'

She looked at Amal. 'He was the most wonderful man I've ever known. He was generous, gentle and kind. I would've loved for you to meet him. You would have liked him.

'I miss him so much. What am I going to do without him?' Her voice cracked and she started to cry. Amal took her mother in her arms.

Inga was a little more skeptical and together with Patrick decided to do a little digging herself. The details they researched about Hakim didn't make for pretty reading. They found his name at the bottom of an old list for being wanted for crimes against humanity. He had been responsible for many deaths it seemed. She shuddered, especially when she recalled the documentary about the mass graves that were unearthed beside Abu Ghraib Prison after the Second Gulf War. They decided unanimously to keep this information from Nazreen. She'd been through enough. Why add to her grief when she just lost the love of her life? Maybe they could tell her when she was a little stronger but what was going to be the point?

'Hi, honey.' Libby breezes into the shed like a breath of fresh air. 'I've given the burgers to Jon. Can you please pour me a large Bacardi and Coke, babe?' she says to Inga and plonks herself on the sofa next to Nazreen.

'Wonderful to see you're out of hospital. I'm Libby. How are you?'

Nazreen holds out her hand to her daughter, beaming with pride at the look of her child and pulls her next to her on the couch.

'I've never been happier,' she says to Libby.

THE END